BLOOD JUSTICE

It began when Kyle Jaeger stole the Strolling B herd and slaughtered five innocent boys at Salvation Creek. It ended in a town in old Mexico, when Freeman and Cobb caught up with the Jaeger gang. Facing their deadly enemies, the gunmen set out to avenge the Strolling B. Behind them stretched a trail soaked in the blood of both hunters and hunted, and the partners were destined to become legends in the history of old Mexico.

Books by Chad Hammer
in the Linford Western Library:

HONDO COUNTY GUNDOWN

CHAD HAMMER

BLOOD JUSTICE

Complete and Unabridged

LINFORD
Leicester

First published in Great Britain in 2005 by
Robert Hale Limited
London

First Linford Edition
published 2006
by arrangement with
Robert Hale Limited
London

British Library CIP Data

Hammer, Chad
    Blood justice.—Large print ed.—
Linford western library
1. Western stories
2. Large type books
I. Title
823.9′2 [F]

ISBN 1-84617-320-5

Published by
F. A. Thorpe (Publishing)
Anstey, Leicestershire

Set by Words & Graphics Ltd.
Anstey, Leicestershire
Printed and bound in Great Britain by
T. J. International Ltd., Padstow, Cornwall

This book is printed on acid-free paper

1

The Godless Breed

The hammer of racing hoofbeats rang loud in the New Mexico night. To both north and south of the racing riders stood the brooding barricades of the ironstone cliffs; ahead the promise of wider country beckoned — broad sweeps of timber-fringed cattle-range shelving steeply downwards to Big River and their ultimate destination, the cowtown of Durant.

Behind them somewhere — trouble.

Tight-jawed astride his outsized sorrel, big Buck Cobb spat out the stub of a brown-paper quirly and shot a hard stare across at his saddle pard as Freeman swerved his black to avoid a yawning gopher hole.

'Know what that moon yonder says, pilgrim?' the young giant bawled above

1

dimming hoof-echoes as the cliffs began to drop away behind.

'You tell me!'

'It says nigh midnight, is what!'

'So?'

'So — for the first time in three years we look likely to miss out on our memorial to the boys in Durant, is what. And who in hell's fault is that?'

The senior of the pair by a couple of years, lean-bodied Luke Freeman chose to delay his reply until the lathered horses had carried them across the wide alkali steppe which gave way abruptly on to the trail leading steeply down.

And suddenly there was cattle-country. Springfield Valley stretched below them, the frail circle of winking lights pinpointing the town by the river.

'What are you griping about?' he retorted. He pointed. 'See for yourself, the place is still wide awake. Five'll get you ten, Matt and the folks are still firing on down there on account they know we'll show sooner

2

or later. Just like always!'

'We'd have been there on sundown and right on time if you hadn't got yourself tangled up with that female back there at Vico Estolo. What the hell were you thinking? The goddamn sheriff's wife!'

Freeman just grinned. Cobb was sore as a boil but he would get over it. So too would the sheriff — most likely. But he offered no apology for badly timed 'romance' which had seen the partners forced to take cover from an enraged peace officer and his deputies for several hours before they were able to fork leather and ride, with horsemen in their distant dust.

Never explain and never apologize. That was just one of the self-made rules this high-living Arizonan elected to live by. He found it saved time and trouble in his often hectic journey through life. Even so, he knew he would feel guilty as hell inside if they were too late now that the pursuit had, at last, dropped off. The annual pilgrimage to Durant on 30 June was about as close as it could be to something sacred in the lives of Buck Cobb and Luke Freeman: Arizonans, cattle-dealers, sometime soldiers of fortune, and one-time trail partners.

There was no shortage of memories as played-out horses carried them past the first of the darkened houses and on towards the lights. They'd been young and eager new partners in the beef business three years earlier, having recently combined their talents to organize and conduct drives north to the railhead, with the big Strolling B ranch here their newest customers.

With five successful major drives behind them, the Strolling B contract promised to be about the easiest and least complicated, would have been but for what happened at a place called Salvation Creek.

The Salvation Creek massacre and the good men who'd survived it were the reason Freeman and Cobb had come so far to be now closing in on

4

the lamplit council chambers of Durant, where the rows of rigs and buggies and tie-racked horses told them Cobb was right. They weren't too late after all.

They were greeted at the door. Coming in from the night into the brightly lit chamber where every remembered face turned eagerly towards them, even the urbane Freeman seemed momentarily off-balanced by the sharp transition from one environment to another.

Then mayor and Strolling B boss Jefferson was striding towards them, right hand outstretched, saying all the right words.

'Knew you'd make it, boys . . . nobody had any doubt.' He pumped their hands and patted each man on the back with tears in his eyes. 'And by God and by glory it wouldn't have been the same without you. OK, your seats are up front and now you're here the reverend can get started.'

The ceremony was simplicity itself,

comprising brief and emotional testimonials to the five baby-faced cowboys from Jefferson's Strolling B Ranch, murdered that night at Salvation Creek by a man named Jaeger, and brought vividly to mind here through the lifesize enlargement by photographer Lucius J. Fry of the picture he'd taken of the wide-eyed quintet the day before the ill-fated drive set out, now ornamenting the wall above the stage.

Cobb and Freeman were seasoned men of the West with no time for sentimentality and little for weakness of any kind. Yet they'd been affected on both occasions prior to this 30 June ritual conducted in this place, and were so again. But something which was beginning to rile them by the time the ceremony drew to a close was the attitude of some of their fellow-mourners. There were men and women here, several of whom had lost sons on that Sangre de Cristo drive, who appeared visibly more excited than sad tonight, and touchy Freeman was on the point of rebuking them as they broke for the traditional coffee and cake.

He was glad he wasn't given that chance when Mayor Jefferson banged on the polished table for silence. Every face in the room turned to the Arizonans with an air of expectancy, which they found passing strange.

'What's going on?' Cobb growled uneasily. His scowl cut deep. 'Is this a memorial or a goddamn shindig?'

'Forgive us if we might seem kinda irreverent, big fella,' said Jefferson. 'But the point is we got a reason for being double and treble grateful that you fellas made it tonight on account we got us some news.'

'Big news, and you ain't gonna believe it,' cut in the cattle-dealer. 'From Sonora.'

Freeman and Cobb exchanged frowns. It was a long time since Sonora had held any significance for them. And the fact that several mourners were now openly smiling sure didn't clarify anything.

'What?' Freeman demanded in his best trail-boss voice.

'He's been sighted, boys,' Jefferson said in a sudden rush. 'The butcher you boys hunted across Mexico for six months after Salvation Creek.' He spread his hands. 'Don't you understand? Kyle Jaeger's alive and was sighted by a man we can trust at Palo Pinto Canyon, Sonora, just days ago!'

Jaeger!

The name hit like a thunderbolt. Even before their eyes met and locked, both Buck Cobb and Luke Freeman knew that the former would not be returning to the huge cattle drive he'd left in the north-west, nor the latter to his beef-packing business up in Colorado.

Without a word passing between them, each knew they would be heading south-west for Sonora before first light.

★   ★   ★

It had been blazing hot that day a week earlier at Palo Pinto Canyon when the blocky little timber-cutter suddenly realized he was going to die — and wanted so desperately to live.

'No!' he cried as the gringo gunman curled back the hammer of his sixgun with deliberate slowness. '*Por favor, señor*, you do not have to kill us!'

Nudging Dold McCrow, the gun-fondling Cady grinned broadly.

'You hear that, pard? The runt claims we got no reason to kill him.'

'Who needs a reason?'

McCrow was also smirking in the shadow of his hat-brim as the trio of Mexican workers stood trembling before them. As was Littleman. The very attitude of the gun-toting trio, which had seemingly appeared from nowhere just as the axemen were breaking for siesta, was chillingly menacing.

'Guess you're just slow to *comprende*, greaser.' Struther Cady was tall and angular with a five-day growth. 'It ain't that we want to gun you boys, it's just that we gotta. Ain't that so, pards?'

McCrow and Littleman nodded but were no longer smiling. '*Por favor* — why?' gasped the tall Mexican. 'What have we done?'

'You boys is cutting timber for the railroad,' stated yellow-eyed Cady. 'Railroads mean progress, and progress just don't set well with the men who sent us here. *Sabe?*'

'Tell you what,' gangling McCrow said suddenly, slipping his .45 into leather and folding lean arms. 'Let's give these good ol' boys a sporting chance.' He nodded. 'Make it to your wagon afore we can count ten and we'll give you a sporting chance to get your rifles and make a fair fight of it. Well, what you waiting for?'

The timber-cutters stood frozen. McCrow and Littleman chuckled in the heat-stricken stillness.

It seemed an interminable time before the runty Mexican broke and ran for the wagon. Instantly the

10

beanpole wheeled and rushed after him, overtaking him in just a few strides. But the third man, dark and powerful in his loose-fitting working smock, refused to play the game.

Instead he lowered his head and charged like a bull. He almost reached McCrow before the outlaw realized his danger. His draw was lightning-fast but even so he still needed three shots to bring the man down, then was forced to jump aside to avoid the falling body.

'Yeehahhh!' Cady howled excitedly, and both men filled their hands to send a storming volley after the runners, still well short of their objective.

The pistols continued to snarl until hammers spun on empty chambers. The echoes rolled and muttered away until the midday seemed suddenly hollow, sucked of all sound

Rawboned Dold McCrow noisily blew smoke from his gun barrel.

'Some loco ideas you get, Cady. That heavyweight danged-nigh got you. OK, let's go see if they got anything in that wagon worth taking while we wait for Jaeger to show, whenever the hell that might be.'

Cordite smoke drifted lazily in the air as the killers slouched for the wagon. Its tendrils wisped their silent way up and over the rim where the terrified desert rat was bellying swiftly backwards out of sight, eyes glazed with the horror of what he'd seen.

Once clear of the rim, Gimpy Jack rose in a half-crouch and ran to his mule on shaky legs. He heaved himself into the saddle, and put boots to rib-cage, darting fearful glances back over his shoulder.

With lonely months in the Mexican desert behind him, Gimpy had deliberately strayed towards 'civilized' country in search of a little human society, desperate for someone to talk to besides Martha.

He still craved company, but wasn't that lonesome.

He'd travelled several miles before

calming enough to realize the enormous significance of what that tall killer had said about waiting for someone named Jaeger.

* * *

The flame of sunset dimmed on the hilltops of Trinity County and dusk was creeping through the sycamores and willows along Riata Creek as the two tall men rode down to make camp. A blue heron cleared the water and winged away through the trees, and a fat grey cottontail hopped lazily into a hollow log.

That was the rabbit's first mistake, for these were hungry men with long miles behind them. It made its second a minute later when Luke kicked one end of the log with his high-heeled riding-boot and it shot out the other — straight into the gut-line slip-noose that Buck Cobb dangled over the exit.

A swift jerk, then the cottontail was

promptly skinned, cleaned, washed, trimmed and curled up neatly in a pan with a plump onion and half a pound of wild potatoes.

'Neat trick that,' Freeman drawled, putting the finishing touches to the fire he'd got going.

'One my daddy taught me,' grinned the husky young giant, hefting the pot.

'I should have guessed . . . your father being such a gold-plated wonder at everything under the sun.'

The badinage was an unconscious attempt to recreate the rapport they'd once shared as partners in the cattle-trade. Before the one drive that had gone tragically wrong, resulting in the eventual split.

Following the slaughter of the Strolling B hands north of Albuquerque that fateful year, the partners had undertaken a punishing manhunt for Kyle Jaeger which had seen them criss-cross northern Sonora over several months before being forced to call it quits. Since then they'd only met twice at the

14

previous memorials in Durant, and both were aware they would have gone their separate ways again on this occasion but for a wire to Jefferson from an old acquaintance named Gimpy Jack.

For three years each man had worked and progressed on his separate path, but neither ever forgot Jaeger or his crime. And now, out of nowhere, had come a possible genuine lead.

Freeman grunted and set about off-saddling his black and Cobb's sorrel. He affixed the hobbles, then drew a silver cigar-case from an inside pocket as he crossed to the fire to sniff the cooking rabbit appreciatively.

He hunkered down to pluck a burning stick from the fire and applied it to cigar tip.

Although cattle-trading and trail-driving were his principal interests, Luke Freeman was a sometime gambler, adventurer and a handy man with a six-shooter, with a flamboyant style and a keen interest in handsome women, characteristics which guaranteed he attracted more than his share of trouble.

The meal was soon ready, yet neither man could muster much of an appetite. Cobb kept rising from his log to check the horses and prowl round the perimeter. He just couldn't seem to settle. Freeman glanced up as the big man returned to the fireglow.

'We should have known, I guess,' he remarked after a silence.

'What? That Jaeger would still be alive, you mean?'

'That breed is always hard to kill.'

'And they mostly take good men with them when they do go.'

'Yeah, good men . . . '

It was three years to the month since they'd driven the herd earmarked for the Fourth Cavalry, CSA — Confederate States of America — up north across New Mexico making for the Sangre de Cristo mountains where the Fighting Fourth was locked in battle with the Yankees.

To make it through to Santa Fe the drive had had to negotiate Gloriette Pass and Apache Canyon, both ideal spots for a Bluecoat ambush.

That night saw Freeman and Cobb forced to quit the herd to drive Strolling B boss Jefferson back to the nearest village, burning up with yellow fever. They had no option but to leave the cattle in charge of five teenage boys off the ranch. Upon their return they found four of them murdered and the fifth dying from gunshot wounds. But for the dying boy's last whispers they might never have known that the leader of the marauders had been identified by his own men as Kyle Jaeger, notorious killer, mercenary leader and former Border Ruffian from Missouri.

The six-month manhunt through Sonora followed. Either Jaeger was a wraith or will-o'-the-wisp who simply could not be tracked down or, they hoped, was dead, rotting someplace with the giant Mexican *zopilote* picking his bones.

But the guilt didn't die.

The herders butchered at Salvation Creek had been mere boys — too young to wear either blue or grey — bright-eyed youngsters of the Arizonan plains who'd felt safe as chickens in a clutch as they headed north for the battle lands with a pair of veterans like Freeman and Cobb. The guilt of that day would likely stay with them until either they or Jaeger were dead.

They were discussing what they'd do after making contact with Gimpy, when Cobb suddenly stiffened.

'What?' Freeman asked.

'Dunno,' Cobb grunted. But he spoke while rising to his feet with a Colt .45 appearing as if by magic in a big bronzed fist.

By the time he returned several minutes later, Cobb still hadn't seen anything untoward. Yet trail-honed instincts kept nagging him.

He rolled a smoke and told Freeman what he planned to do. Freeman was saddle-weary, the hour was getting late and he could sense nothing out of place in the borderland night. But experience from the old days warned that when big Buck Cobb got one of his hunches it was far easier to go along with him than argue. Experience also confirmed that nine times out of ten, his hunches paid out.

Nothing is as dark as a starless Mexican night. On this particular night the breeze would suddenly rise, then shift uncertainly across the Riata Creek camp, whispering in the trees and brushing the face of the water.

A finger of wind dipped out of the darkness, raised a cloud of powdery ash from the fire and dusted it across the two, blanket-shrouded shapes spread on the earth. It stirred the manes of the horses. Then it fell away and died and the night was hushed again.

But not still.

Not quite, as the dull thud of a rawhide-booted hoof striking rock sounded from somewhere beyond the pale perimeter of firelight.

19

The sorrel tossed its head, the camp-fire reflected in its eyes as he stared in the direction of that faint sound. The blanket-shrouded shapes did not stir. The black stamped nervously. Now there was nothing at all to be heard but the faint burbling of the water, then the whirring beat of wings as an owl sped overhead, hunting.

Silence.

Eventually the vagrant wind started up again, and as though seemingly boosted forward by it, three grey-jacketed figures ghosted out of the shadows into the light. One man halted cautiously by the stream while the other two crept forward. The nightcomers wore no spurs, made no sound as they infiltrated the camp. Firelight winked on gun barrels and burnished hard faces with a soft yellow sheen. The fire popped and they stopped, eyes stabbing at the motionless campers. The sleepers didn't stir and the intruders moved forward again until they could feel the warmth of the embers.

McCrow halted with a silent gesture and stared across at the tethered horses. Quality horseflesh, the very best. The saddles were the very finest also, the sort of saddles a good thief would travel far to find. He hunkered down by the nearest sleeper, with his heavy revolver almost touching the battered hat that covered the man's head, and spoke softly.

'Rise-and-shine time, cowboy.'

No response.

McCrow spoke louder. 'OK, wake up you bastards, you got company.'

Still neither blanket stirred.

Uncertainty stirred McCrow's gaunt features as he uncoiled and glanced at Littleman.

The other shrugged. McCrow reached out with his boot, poked a blanket with his toe. There was a strange sound, like rattling sticks. The hellions traded puzzled looks. Then McCrow bent from the waist and ripped the blanket away.

The bedroll contained nothing but a pile of brush and twigs arranged in a form to resemble a man asleep. There was no head beneath the big hat, just a large rock. McCrow jumped backwards, eyes rolling bright and sick in their sockets as he focused on the second bedroll. Now they could see more than before. This one too was a dummy.

'You gentlemen looking for us?'

The voice came hard and cartridge-clear from a clump of rocks on the north side of the clearing. The hellions whirled, juggling guns, seeking a target

'Drop them shooters!' Buck Cobb's shout erupted from behind a deadfall log across from the rocks. 'We got you cold!'

The intruders' eyes were wild as they realized they were covered from both sides, a deadly situation. But Struther Cady, positioned well back along the bank, felt secure enough to take a chance.

'No, don't!' Freeman shouted as he saw the dimly visible figure jerk up his sixgun. But there was no halting killer

Cady as he cut loose with two shots that thudded into Cobb's deadfall. With no option now, McCrow and Littleman shouted and swung up blazing guns as though unaware of the unmissable targets they made standing almost on top of the bright fire.

As gun-thunder erupted from rocks and log, Littleman staggered, his right hand clutching his chest where bright blood bubbled through his fingers. Reflexes jerked off a final shot before a bullet sent him spinning with his guns flying high, dead before he hit ground.

McCrow didn't see his henchman fall. He was taking huge, long-legged leaps towards the surrounding darkness, with twin guns blazing recklessly, howling something unintelligible at the now invisible Cady.

A lead fusillade smashed him down.

McCrow was as tough as any professional butcher should be. His face ghastly, he got up on one knee and drilled off another shot that smacked a rock and ricocheted, missing Freeman by inches.

Sixguns replied and the killer died in a mad thunderclap of raging sound.

Above the dying echoes came the sound of hoof-beats coming from south of the clearing. Cobb got there first to see two free horses stampeding into the darkness, the third man already gone. The two returned to the camp-fire and stared at the dead.

'Sons of bitches!' Freeman said bitterly, deft fingers reloading hot guns. Then: 'You OK?'

'Fine.'

Cobb didn't sound fine. The former partners had seen plenty gunplay in their time but were never eager to solve problems with sixguns even so. But in situations like this, a man was left without options.

He walked to the first corpse and went through his pockets. No identification. The other proved the same. To the eyes of experts, the dead had the familiar unmistakable looks of the owlhoot about them, hard faces, rough garb, big guns. The one curious thing about them were the grey jackets and black hats of a similar type favoured by the *Rurales* of this region.

Talking it over, they agreed that it was highly unlikely that Americans would be accepted as *Rurales*, particularly outlaws.

They brewed up, then began preparing to move out; they weren't likely to rest any with dead badmen about and at least one live one out there someplace. Cobb was reaching for his bedroll when he suddenly stiffened at a faint sound only a man of the wilds like himself might have heard.

'Down!' he shouted and hit ground with a .45 appearing as if by magic in a big bronzed fist. Freeman rolled and flipped behind a clump of brush. They heard the sound of hoofs from the east, swung in that direction, were primed and ready to open up like siege cannon, when a squeaky nervous voice reached them.

'It's OK, Buck, Luke, it's only me.'

They recognized the voice and their guns were coming down as Gimpy Jack, one-time cook on the ill-fated Strolling B drive to the Sangres, and his mule emerged like ghosts out of the darkness.

Gimpy sat with his back to the dead and slurped up coffee while he told his story. After wiring Durant with his information on the Jaeger sighting in which he offered to wait and meet 'anybody interested' here at Riata Creek, he'd done just that. But while he was holed up in caves a couple of miles south he'd been horrified to see the same bunch of butchers he'd seen in action at Palo Pinto come drifting by.

He'd spent several days hiding in a limestone cavern, only emerging when he figured the danger was gone, and when anybody who might have responded to his wire might well be on their way to Riata.

He'd neither seen nor heard anything untoward until sighting the camp-fire Cobb and Freeman had built in order to attract their would-be informant, and he was heading in that direction astride Martha when the guns began to roar.

It had taken a combination of courage and greed for Gimpy Jack to work his wary way down along the Riata an hour after the guns fell silent. Now he kept looking from one man to the other, needing the reassurance of their company at this grisly spot with two riddled corpses lying almost out of sight in the background.

They listened as he graphically described what he'd witnessed at Palo Pinto canyon.

No, he didn't know why Cady and his hellers had chopped down the railroad timber-cutters in cold blood, he conceded, but he did have a theory.

'Let's hear it,' Freeman said easily.

'I guess you know they've been laying new railroad track from where the North Mexico terminates at Casa Grande?' he queried.

They nodded.

'Well, the word is that someone don't

want the line to go through,' he went on. 'So the way I see it, mebbe Jaeger's gun dogs jumping those fellers cutting railroad ties for the line had something to do with whoever's so dead-set against the railroad goin' ahead.'

'OK, so let's get down to cases, Gimpy,' Cobb said. 'You dead certain the man you seen was Jaeger?'

Gimpy Jack shivered and it had nothing to do with the chill. That night when five boy-men were slain and a five-hundred-head herd of beeves were run off by a pack of gun-hung rustlers, he had lain unseen under a canvas sheet watching with appalled eyes as a tall and powerfully built man urged on his gunmen in their horrific task of murder. The big man had ridden round the corpses slamming bullets into the motionless shapes, yet had still some-how not finished off Tommy Wilson who'd lasted long enough to identify Jaeger before he died.

Gimpy's story was that he'd been away from the camp gathering firewood when the attack came and he'd stuck by it ever since. The truth was the little man was a coward, and there was but one thing that could make him risk danger of any kind, such as he was doing here.

Money.

He cleared his throat and furnished a perfect description of Kyle Jaeger. His listeners knew it fitted the killer to a T from the truebills showing the outlaw's likeness that had proliferated throughout the south-west following Salvation Creek.

If they sensed Gimpy had shown yellow at Salvation Creek, they gave no sign. Jaeger preoccupied them totally.

'OK,' Freeman said at last, rising and pressing a wad of bills into a shaking hand. 'Now, any notion which way Jaeger might have headed from the canyon?'

Gimpy was counting his money.

'I hear whispers. Man like me hears most everything sooner or later . . . '

He paused, eyes wide. Freeman

palmed off another twenty and thrust it at him.

'What?' he rapped.

'Only whispers, Mr Freeman, but I'm told that when Jaeger disappeared for so long he'd took a boat from Mazaltan, then up the coast to San Francisco and worked in the diggings. They say he's been back in Sonora over a year and has been mighty busy doing some pretty big things . . . only I got no idea what, only that it's some place due west.'

'Some place west!' Freeman said disgustedly an hour later as, with the little man long gone, they mounted and rode away from the place of death. 'And I gave him a twenty for that!'

Cobb made no reply. He was already riding ahead searching for sign of the Jaeger man who'd survived.

2

Along the Yaqui Trail

They followed the faint trace of the ancient Yaqui Trail with the sun climbing their backs.

The Sonoran north-west was a strange corner of a region they otherwise knew well, yet Buck Cobb's sense of direction kept them dead on a west by southwest course just as surely as if he'd had a compass set in the swellfork pommel of his big Texas-Spanish saddle.

The terrain slowly changed and grew rougher as the miles drifted behind. Here, eastern Ocotillo Province was a tumbled landscape of rugged rock-bench slopes, brushy hogback ridges and deep-gashed canyons. Occasionally they passed by tight little valleys dotted with piñon and gnarled old oaks.

Cottonwoods, willows and junipers marked the watercourses which were slowly drying up under the midsummer sun.

The morning began overcast and cloudy but the sun forced its way through while they nooned on a rocky cedar-covered ridge, then blazed down at full strength as they pushed on into the afternoon.

'Big country,' Freeman murmured, more to break the silence than to shape comment.

'Big enough.'

They were still a long distance from the old easy rapport that had characterized their earlier years together. But already there were signs that they were loosening up some in one another's company again. Dissimilar in so many ways they still shared common characteristics such as determination and a taste for the new and dangerous.

And, of course, a hunger for justice.

'What'd you make of Gimpy's story on Jaeger, Buck?'

'Well, the Gimp always had a way of blowing things up some, but I reckon most of what he told us might be true. We know one thing. The killings at Palo Pinto and the way those geezers came after us at the creek have sure got the whiff of Jaeger about them.'

'Uh-huh. And what he said about Jaeger being involved in something big down here, that fits in too. We always knew the bastard could organize and lead men, always thought big.' Freeman frowned and pointed. 'Hey, what's that yonder? Looks like a buffalo wallow.'

A buffalo wallow it was, a big one, several hundred yards across. A dozen or more buffalo were rolling in the dust, seeking relief from heat and insects. A rugged young bull with a cowbird perched on one stubby horn rose to its feet and eyed the intruders suspiciously but showed no sign of fear. The others went on rolling and grunting and really enjoying life, at least from a buffalo's point of view.

'Never knew the big shaggies got this

far south in the summer,' Cobb observed, fixing a quirley. 'Must have been driven down by the hide-hunters.'

'Possibly.' Freeman had already forgotten the buffalo. Peering ahead through the sifting dust-veils, his mind was going back to when they'd travelled Sonora before, hunting the same elusive quarry they hunted today, three years on.

Their previous hunt for Jaeger had taken them mainly through the southern and western regions of sprawling Ocotillo Province, only to end in failure. Several times they'd mistakenly thought they had him cornered. But each time Jaeger had proved more than their match, in the process revealing rare cunning, ice-cold nerve and a total ruthlessness.

Kyle Jaeger was certainly no man to be taken lightly and even if they had no reason to expect trouble away out here in the rough country, their close call at Riata Creek ensured both kept sharp.

Cobb pointed south-west past the

wallow where a distant line of low-lying hills were turning purple in the dusk.

'We'll circle this here buffalo waller, then cut straight for yonder fold in them hills. If I don't miss my guess, we should be able to sight the notches of Pierro Pass from there.'

'I'll likely regret asking this,' Freeman drawled, 'but what do you feel about Pierro? What do those mystic instincts of yours — handed down from father to son, of course, tell you about Pierro Pass? In other words, is he there or isn't he? Twenty words or less, if possible.'

Cobb just grinned. 'Wonder what Old Pappy's doing right now while we're shooting up Old Mexico, Freeman?'

'Just yes or no will suffice. Pierro Pass. Pay-dirt or otherwise?'

Cobb sobered, staring ahead.

'OK, serious question, serious answer. I don't know.'

'Don't know? Since when has not knowing stopped you laying opinions and predictions thick on the ground.'

Freeman was looking for a bite but Cobb was serious.

'OK, smart-mouth,' he drawled, 'I'm going for the negative. I don't reckon we'll find him there.'

'Why not?'

They steered their horses across a gully-wash where cicadas set up a deafening racket. Once out of earshot, Cobb said:

'Jaeger's back after a long spell away, maybe just as big or even bigger than before. Likely everyone's about forgot when we chased him through Pierro then down on south. But this corner of Sonora's a mite too close to Arizona and the Rangers for him still.' He nodded. 'Uh-huh. My pappy's instincts tell me we'll have to go deeper to flush him, either west or south.'

By this Freeman had dropped his teasing manner. What he'd heard sounded like good sense. They rode on a spell in silence until Freeman said suddenly:

'Wonder why he did it?'

'Huh?'

'Came back.' He gestured. 'You and I ran him ragged before. We know he jumped ship wounded and in bad shape. The big hero who bragged he'd bury us then go back to the States and take up where he left off, was so worn out and dog-yellow that all he could do was crawl aboard a ship and disappear. Well, it paid off. Once he was on the high seas sailing up the Pacific coast there were just too many possible jumping-off places even for an army of hunters to cover. San Diego, Los Angeles, Santa Monica, 'Frisco, Seattle . . . '

Freeman shook his head.

'Gone. Home free. Then suddenly he's back and up to his old murderous games. Why?

'Maybe he'll tell us when we're hauling him back to Durant and the law,' Freeman grunted.

'Unless he makes us kill him,' he said with sudden steel in his voice.

Cobb's blue eyes swept the limitless landscape. Because of their manhunt here, they knew these mountainous northern regions of Sonora better than most Americans. Knew the ranges and wild rivers, valleys, plains towns, cities and ports — the thousand-and-one places a man could hide — those vast but hidden places where you could conceal a regiment.

Even so, this time they would follow their quarry no matter what. They hadn't said so but each man knew it.

From where the trail switchbacked over a series of broken ridges lined with cottonwoods, they squinted against the glare and stared ahead several miles to where a low range gapped the skyline distinctively with stone jaws.

It was the pass.

Pierro Pass they knew well from yet another false trail they'd once followed down from Nogales and across the Rio Arriba. Freeman immediately perked up at the prospect of seeing it again. Although he made his living bossing cattle drives with all the dangers and hardship that that involved, he still couldn't get enough of towns, good times, pretty women and the sort of mostly innocent trouble that accompanied such simple pleasures.

Gigging his long-legged black forward, he led the way down off the ridgeline beyond which lay a clearly marked trail which took them on uneventfully all the way to Pierro Pass and trouble.

3

Jaeger Country

'Some chilli perhaps, *señor*?'

Cobb hefted his sack of supplies. 'Reckon not.'

'You do not like chilli con carne?'

'Matter of fact I'm right partial, *amigo*. But the fact is I've got a trail partner who's kinda leery of Mex chow.'

The little man behind the counter shrugged philosophically.

'It is sad when one encounters such a thing. But you are an *Americano* of taste, are you not?'

'Well, I dunno about that. But I know what I like, and I sure do like tortillas and frijoles and such almost as much as baked ham and rye hominy.'

'And tamales, you like tamales?'

'*Señor*, you're looking at a tamale-eating champeen.'

'*Uno momento.*'

The man vanished in back, returning immediately bearing a cornmeal tube filled with spicy red meat.

'The compliments of Jose Augustin, *señor.*'

Cobb accepted the tamale and chewed off half with one bite. He munched appreciatively. '*Señor,* this is one fine tamale. I thank you kindly.'

'You're welcome.' Cobb fingered the remainder of the spicy food into his mouth, slung his possibles sack over his shoulder and left.

He walked out to the sorrel at the rack, dozing in the sun. Cobb looped the sack rope round the pommel of his big Texas-Spanish saddle. He built a smoke and leaned back against the tooth-chewed hitch rail and watched life in Pierro Pass go by.

The town was poor and down-at-heel. He shrugged and asked himself if that was his problem. The answer was no. He had just one problem and it had an American name. Kyle Jaeger.

Yet walking the horse down the side street he felt easier, aware that despite the pervading air of hardship Pierro Pass still had a satisfying appeal about it, a slice of old-time Mexican life, of sun-soaked adobe and dappled tree-shade.

The sorrel nudged his shoulder for titbits as he led it past a produce stall and on towards the central square and the Casa Grande, where Freeman was waiting across from a building identified by a gate sign as an office of the *Nuevos Rurales*.

He figured the '*Nuevos*' *Rurales* must have sprung up since they last were in Sonora. They didn't look any smarter or more honest than the old *Rurales*.

So — why should he worry?

He wasn't aware that the shrug of big, blue-shirted shoulders caught the eye of an American emerging from a store directly opposite the Casa Grande, clutching a sack of tobacco. Immediately the man propped and stepped back into the shadow of the building.

Twenty hours earlier Struther Cady had watched in a fever of fear and guilt as he saw his pards shot down by two Arizonans whom he'd last sighted more than two years ago as they had hounded Cady and the Jaeger bunch half-way across Sonora!

'Cobb!' the man gasped, then half-fell backwards through a doorway as innocent-seeming blue eyes flicked in his direction.

There was no risk of his being recognized under those circumstances, and the moment Cobb passed from sight, Cady re-emerged and dashed for the livery stable, leaking sweat at every stride.

Frijoles and cold beer were a speciality of the house at the Casa Grande, and although his palate was attuned to a classier cuisine, Freeman was tucking into his second helping as Cobb appeared, seeming to dwarf everyone in sight as he shoved through the batwings.

'Off your chow?' Buck grinned, filling an empty chair.

'Order you some?'

Cobb fingered his hat off his forehead and tilted his chair to its back legs.

'Strange to say I ain't hungry.'

'Last night affecting your appetite, maybe?'

'Maybe. It's the old story. But so soon as Jaeger's name comes up anyplace there's always killing just around the corner. That was how it was before, how it is again.' Cobb sighed and looked up. 'Hear anything fresh on him yet?'

'Depends.'

Cobb's scowl cut deep.

'What the hell is that supposed to mean?'

'What it means, I guess, is that I'm not hearing what I expected to hear.'

'Look, if you figure I'll sit here listening to you run off at the mouth without saying anything, Joe College — '

'OK, OK, don't get your back up. What I'm hearing about Jaeger makes him sound changed some from before. For example, would you believe I've been told by the locals here that he's regarded as a man of high standing and substance in Grande Ronde?'

'You sure about that?'

'That girl yonder is dead certain he definitely rides on the high side of the street now. Seems he's got money to burn, bosses some kind of a bunch, is still in and out of trouble but apparently now has strong connection with the *Rurales* — '

'Whoa there! In with the John Laws? Jaeger?'

'You think it sounds loco. So do I. But it seems whatever's happened to Jaeger since we camped on his trail has changed him.'

'No matter what kind of respectable hat he might be wearing now, he's still what he always was underneath.'

'A cold-blooded killer.' Freeman's expression was cold as sleet for a moment. 'Of course. What I'm trying to figure is exactly what we're up against, is all. Suddenly I'm getting this picture of a wised-up Jaeger who's moved up in the world. We could be taking on something far bigger than we figured, cowboy.'

'So?' Cobb's expression was pugnacious.

Freeman replied with a quick grin. 'But did that ever bother Freeman and Cobb — Cattle Dealers?'

'Not for five goddamn minutes.'

Freeman nodded and for a moment it was just like the old days when the firm of Freeman and Cobb would agree on tackling something crazy, like driving 1500 head from Canada to Montana during the blizzard season — without a moment's doubt or hesitation. Back before the massacre and the haunting guilt.

Cobb had just slowly fashioned a cigarette and set it between his teeth, when a slender hand holding a light appeared before him and he looked up into the twinkling dark eyes of Carmelita, the girl Freeman had pointed out.

The girl torched his smoke into life, he inhaled and grinned.

'Much obliged, ma'am.' He watched her ripple away thoughtfully. 'You reckon maybe we're taking life too serious tonight, Joe College?'

'Were, but not any longer,' the other responded, snapping erect. 'Not tonight, leastways. Lets go hit the tables and see if we can't stir up some real action that's not of the hurting kind. And I reckon we could sure do worse than look up the Hogan girls, don't you?'

'The Hogan girls ... ' Freeman's look was far away. He nodded briskly. 'You're right. Tomorrow can look after itself.'

★   ★   ★

Kyle Jaeger led his riders towards the crumbling edifice of the old brick *torreón* atop Mesa Zemora a little after moonrise.

With the well-drilled habits of men who spent their lives on the trail on horseback, the dozen and more American guntoters attended to their mounts while the man appointed cook for the day built a fire out of driftwood and brush. With the flames soon lighting up the scarred and ancient walls of the old look-out tower that had been erected here during the fierce Apache wars, the man loaded his skillets up with meat and pone bread and somehow managed to juggle three big coffee-pots into the coals before breaking out tin plates and cutlery.

Gringo Jaeger's core gang, known in places as the Jaegermen, were skilled and efficient campers. Even so every man was looking forward eagerly to reaching Grande Ronde where they'd 'camp' in the premier hotel and dine at the best eateries as befitted their status before returning to their permanent base on one of the plushest Spanish ranches in the province.

Jaeger was a big man, six-three in handmade boots of Spanish leather, a wide-shouldered and powerfully featured product of the wild places of the West with shoulder-length hair as black as any Mexican's, trim-waisted and flat of hips which were encircled by belted twin walnut-butted six-shooters snugly seated in cutaway leather holsters.

Red-headed Wolf Tierney, although well over six feet himself and strongly moulded, seemed almost small by comparison. But in terms of ability and temperament there was little distinction between the pair. Each had ridden on the shady side of the trail all their lives, both were veterans of the Border Ruffians of bloody Missouri, the guerilla wars in New Mexico and, two and a half years earlier, the flight to California which had seen them eventually return a year later to pursue Jaeger's reawakened ambition. Tierney had little ambition other than to stay alive, indulge his every passion and stand by his leader, the one man he admired above all others.

California had saved Jaeger's life after he was forced to flee there from Mexico and manhunters Freeman and Cobb. Even so, he'd arrived at the diggings wounded, broke and desperate, hoping only to survive — when something happened.

Standing shivering in the ice-cold Maverick Mountain mining-camp creek fifty miles north-west of Placerville with nothing in his pockets and a great buffeting gale soaring in from the Pacific setting his teeth to aching, he had hit total rock-bottom for the first time in his life.

Then he bounced.

Stripped down to hard-edged reality by hard times, pain and defeat, the outlaw was suddenly seeing things with crystal-clear vision — saw how far lesser men than Kyle Jaeger employed craft, guile and ruthlessness to take advantage of a given situation in order to climb the ladder of success.

In particular had been the case of the mine bosses who owned the only genuine gold-bearing claim in fifty miles. While Jaeger was working for these men as bodyguard, he fell into the company of a bunch of Welsh rascals whom he befriended, then studied like an avid scientist as they first cleaned out the owners, then eventually dumped their bodies at the bottom of a mine shaft and took over their leases just as easy as ABC, afterwards employing bluff, threats, bribes and graft to ensure that their new ownership was never properly investigated. At last sighting they had been living like kings.

Their take-over had Jaeger suddenly recalling a place called the Valley of the Dons in Sonora, where he was a kind of hero to a rich *jefe de rancho*, where two or three Dons held dubious title to some of the finest grazing land in the region which stood at a vast 200 miles distance from the seat of government and the law. In that moment of recollection he conceived, developed and eventually acted upon a plan that could remove him from the perilous path of the owlhoot and ultimately see him installed as a mighty land baron, rich, honoured and untouchable.

So began the resurrection which had ultimately led him to quit the States and return quietly to Sonora a changed man fired on ambition.

From that point on the climb had been swift and exhilarating. Right at that moment he was savouring every ounce of his advancement and ever-growing power as he bit off the tip of a black cheroot and allowed black eyes to drift from his foot-soldiers and play over the landscape sprawled beneath an open sky.

He lighted up, drew deeply on the bitter smoke and spat a tobacco fragment from the corner of his mouth.

Below him lay beautiful mesquite riverbed country which rolled away into the west until fading out amongst the giant stone toes and brooding massive-ness of the Big Bosque range which enclosed rich and fertile Saragoza Valley, more commonly known as the Valley of the Dons.

He smiled thinly as he thought in turn of Don Patricio, Don Valdez and Don D'Palma the former bitter enemies but now more like partners — thanks largely to Jaeger, the conciliator. Then a less benign thought intruded and he turned to his *segundo* at his side.

'Any word on Cady?'

'Nothing.'

'Not since they hit the railroaders?'

'Not since then.'

'They better have damn good reason to be tardy,' Jaeger gestured impatiently. 'Go tell the boys to be ready to ride in fifteen minutes.'

'I guess some of them are pretty played out, Kyle.'

'So?'

When Jaeger used that tone even Tierney buttoned up. He moved off, barking instructions.

Although most of those assembled at the mesa had been riding with the band ever since his return, none outside Tierney had any comprehension of the full extent of Jaeger's ever widening involvements and interests. A gang member would be assigned certain tasks, invariably of a violent or criminal nature, and would either complete them or die in the attempt without understanding why.

The anomaly of gringo outlaws riding roughshod over Mexican and Indian slave workers, as they did in the valley, frequently led to resentment and rebellion, pathetic uprisings which were invariably put down by the alien 'Jaegermen'.

Jaeger himself was rarely involved in such skirmishes, having absorbed the lessons of his failure, flight, resurrection and return only too well. Once the mad dog heller with a gun who attracted every ugly headline, this new man was now most often cast in the role of impresario and the puppeteer working behind the scenes who could cause his puppets either to dance or die according to his whim.

Dusk was descending by the time Tierney finished briefing several hard-bitten squad leaders, and followed the lackey now leading Jaeger's appaloosa across to him, when a look-out called down from the *torreón*.

'Rider comin' from the north! Could be Cady!'

'Son of a bitch!' Jaeger growled, waving the horseboy away. 'Now he shows, days late.' He cocked a black eyebrow at Tierney as the dust from the approaching horseman blew up and over the mesa rim. 'Seems to me that pilgrim's been getting sloppy recent. It just could be coming on culling time for Struther.' He paused as the rider topped out the plateau. 'And why aren't McCrow and Littleman with him?'

'He's likely got good reason for showing up overdue, Kyle.' Tierney couldn't care less what befell Cady. But as it was his duty to muster the manpower for their various gun jobs, he didn't want to see a top gun canned or killed just for busting a few rules. Nine times out of ten, Cady got the job done. In this organization that talent rated high.

'Hau, boss!' Cady greeted, lifting his right hand palm forward in the Indian-style peace greeting as he reined in. 'Look, before you start in on a man, Kyle, I gotta tell you — '

'Where's McCrow and Littleman?' Jaeger barked. 'And how come the three of you weren't here when I rode in like I ordered? Better talk fast, mister.'

Struther Cady did just that, and a hush fell over the outlaw ranks as they heard how both lanky McCrow and rugged Littleman were now riding the Boot Hill Express.

'How and who?' In the dying light, Jaeger's features resembled something stamped out of bronze.

Cady swallowed. His palms were damp. The first fleabites of fear and concern had begun attacking him on the ride out to the rendezvous — now they spread into a nettlerash of acute anxiety.

'You ain't gonna like this, boss — '

'Damn you!' Jaeger barked, but as Tierney started menacingly forward Cady responded fast.

'It was them, boss. The geezers from Salvation Creek. Freeman and Cobb. What's more, the sons of bitches are down in Pierro Pass right now, swaggering about like gamecocks, large as life — larger mebbe.'

Freeman and Cobb!

In a moment the mesa went quiet as a stopped clock, Jaeger's voiceless rage swirling in the air like smoke.

Few of this bunch had been with Jaeger three summers ago at Salvation Creek, New Mexico. But all knew the story of what happened there and of how Jaeger had been chased out of the States by two relentless cattlemen and hounded like a wild animal through the mountains of Sonora for half a year before being forced to jump a northbound windjammer to save himself.

None had heard a word of Freeman and Cobb since, and even Tierney felt uneasy at the way Jaeger just went on staring fixedly at Cady, who looked back wildly, not knowing if his piece of news might cost him his life.

Then: 'OK.'

Everybody blinked and relaxed a little at that, astonished by how calm Jaeger suddenly appeared as he flipped a coin and caught it.

'Goes without saying they put McCrow and Littleman in the ground, I guess?'

'Yo, boss.' Cady was leaking the cold sweat of relief.

Jaeger faced the north.

'What did you make of those two down at the pass?' he asked. 'Were they in a hurry-up, or taking it easy.'

'Er . . . looked like they was taking their time, Kyle.' Cady's head bobbed. 'Uh-huh, the big fella was leading a hoss when I sighted him, just slouching along and making for Hogan's Hotel, so he was. I never seen Freeman, but a geezer told me that flash bastard's there large as life, likely bragging it up about blowing my brave boys into sawdust . . . Kyle . . . ?'

Jaeger walked away. He kept on until reaching a nest of grey boulders standing together like ancient totems on the rim of the mesa slope on its northern (or Pierro Pass) side.

Nobody spoke. It seemed the whole plateau was quiet when it really wasn't. Minutes dragged by. No one knew what to expect as Jaeger eventually turned and came back.

'Take them all to the Rio Arriba,' he calmly said to Tierney. 'I'll meet you at the camp at sun-up.'

'What . . . what are you going to do, boss?' Tierney asked hesitantly.

'My business.'

'But, Kyle — '

'Dust!'

* * *

The piano and squeeze-box cranked up a tune and a voluptuous Mexican girl appeared on the stage. There was little of the cantina girls' brashness about her and it seemed plain she was uncomfortable in the silver-sequinned dress that bared both her shoulders and the silky roundness of her upper breasts.

She began to sing in an untrained voice about a Mexican *vaquero* named Miguel who was lonesome for home. She wasn't good, but to Joe Cobb, nursing a beer, and Luke Freeman, nursing a buxom percenter, her honesty and sweet shyness made that seem unimportant.

But the lean American with the drunken, bloated face suddenly saw himself as music critic as he got noisily to his feet at the next table and slammed his beer mug down hard.

'Back to slinging hash, girlie! You sing like a crow with a bad throat.'

The music stopped. The girl broke off, her hand fluttering to her throat.

'Bring on the dancing girls!' hollered

the drunk. 'Let's see something for our money.'

Heavy steps sounded in the mounting quiet. A blue shirt-sleeve blurred and a ham of a fist exploded against the drunk's chin and sat him down sharply on the seat of his britches.

Cobb sucked his knuckles. 'The lady is trying to sing, peckerhead.'

The drunk had nothing further to say. He simply sat there with eyes rolled back and mouth hanging agape in a fool's grin.

Cobb's stare ran challengingly over the silent crowd. Then he signalled to the stage.

'Pardon the interruption, ma'am.'

The musicians struck up, the girl began to sing hesitantly and Cobb returned to his table. He hefted his glass and Freeman saw the white hood of undercut flesh where his knuckles had made contact with the drinker's snaggled teeth.

He drew on his cigar and watched the drunk's friends tote him out.

'While I admire the gallantry,' he said quietly, 'I suggest you tone it down a little. No point in drawing attention to ourselves under the circumstances.'

Cobb set his heavy jaw stubbornly.

'He begged for it and he got it.'

Freeman let it lie. No one could be more obdurate than Cobb when his sensibilities were affronted. Freeman was also aware that his partner was still tense in the wake of the killings at Riata Creek. Then there was the suspicion that they were now hunting a Jaeger who might prove to be far stronger and more dangerous than anticipated. The uncertainty of this plainly bothered Cobb and might have done so with Freeman if he wasn't enjoying himself so much.

Once she resumed the singer's performance improved as she went along. When she finished, the two Americans applauded so enthusiastically that Freeman's girl got up and flounced away in a jealous huff. The singer smiled in their direction. Still nervous, she made her way between the tables for the dressing-room when a soft voice sounded behind the Arizonans.

'The *Americanos* would appear to be music-lovers.'

They turned to confront a middle-aged Mexican gentleman, slender and clean-shaven but for a dash of a pencil-line moustache. He wore a dapper officer's uniform with insignia on the sleeves, and his hair was shiny black and brushed straight back from his forehead.

'Captain Melgosa of the *Veintiuno Contreras Province Federales* at your service, gentlemen. May I join you?'

'Well, seeing as we can't seem to attract any women tonight . . . ' Cobb drawled, shoving out a chair with a big boot. 'Take the weight off. Captain, you say?'

'A visitor to Ocotillo Province,' they were informed as the man took a chair. He placed his smart billed cap upon the table and studied them keenly before speaking again. 'I'll be frank, gentle-men. The purpose of my visit to Ocotillo is to look into and eventually produce a report on the state of law and order here for the *Federales*.'

'How does that concern us?' Free-man asked innocently.

'I'm advised you have just arrived from the East. Is that not correct?'

They nodded and he went on:

'Just tonight I received a report of several killings in the Palo Pinto Canyon region. It occurred to me that you gentlemen may have seen or heard something in your travels . . . '

'Negative,' said Freeman, and Cobb added, 'Nothin'.'

To their surprise, the captain smiled.

'Exactly what I expected you to say.' He spread his hands. 'Who would not?' Then serious again, he said, 'You are not total strangers to Sonora and Pierro Pass, so I understand?'

They traded glances.

'We've been here before,' Freeman conceded. No point in lying when there were people here who knew them from their visit two and half years back.

'Hunting a man named Jaeger, if I am correctly informed?'

'Hunted him then, hunting him now,' Cobb growled. 'And if you want to make something of that, mister, you might recollect that Jaeger went through your *Contreras'* Province maybe several times in all while we were chasing him without you *Federales* ever offering to join in. So we failed and you failed. But now we're on the hunt again and we ain't gonna fail, so what do you make of that?'

Captain Melgosa studied them in silence. At close quarters he was aware of their formidable aura. He also noted that both held their hands below the table line, where for all he knew they could be holding sixguns trained on his belly.

But rough stuff or danger didn't faze this cool captain. He was a proficient and highly regarded officer of the law currently engaged upon a difficult and possibly dangerous assignment. His smile appeared almost genuine.

'What I propose to do, if you will permit me, gentlemen, is to buy you both a drink.'

They didn't object. There was something almost likeable about this dapper little officer. They also were quick to suspect that, due to his position and rank, he might possibly prove able to supply information that could benefit them in their hunt.

The hour that followed passed comfortably and it wasn't until the captain rose to leave that his veneer of affability seemed to fade

'Señor Cobb, Señor Freeman, I have much enjoyed your company as well as your disarming frankness. But the fact of the matter is there is major upheaval and unrest in this province at the moment and part of my reason for being here is to seek out the root causes, make recommendations to my superiors and then do whatever I might to defuse the situation. That said, I will be honest. You gentlemen impress, but I'm acutely aware that you seem anything but reassuring. In short, I think Ocotillo would be better off without you and your mission, which even if successful must only cause more violence. Would you be offended if I asked you to take your manhunt elsewhere?'

'Deeply,' Freeman said in a steely voice.

Cobb stared up at the man with a weighted gaze.

'Double offended here.'

'In other words — '

'In other words,' Freeman cut in, 'if you did your job right, you might even get to Jaeger and deal with him before we do. Somehow I don't like your chances.'

The captain was pale but controlled.

'In that case, *señors*,' he said with a slight bow and a sharp click of heels, '*gracias* for your company, and *buenos noches*.'

They watched the slender, erect

figure move along the bar to signal for a tequila.

'What do you reckon?' Freeman asked.

'Probably more than he looks . . . ' He broke off as he saw the girl in the sequinned dress approaching. 'How do, little lady. Join us?'

'I just wanted to thank you for what you did earlier, *señor*,' she replied, dimpling at Cobb. 'For enabling me to complete my performance.'

'Shucks, 'tweren't nothing, ma'am.'

'Our pleasure,' Freeman supported, rising with a smile. 'Would you do us the honour of joining us for a drink?'

The next hour winged by. They found the girl every bit as charming and innocent as she appeared to be; it was surprising, in the wake of the sort of brutal violence they'd unleashed at Riata Creek, just how appealing a lovely woman could be.

At another time and place the evening might have finished up with open conflict between the two over who should escort her home. But not tonight, and for a very good reason.

The manhunters had a prior engagement.

On their arrival they'd checked into the only accommodation in town run by an American. They'd stayed over with local identity Pop Hogan at his sturdy Hogan's Hotel previously.

The hospitality at Pop's was first rate, his table as fine as anything you'd encounter north of the border — but his daughters were definitely not on the menu.

At least that had been the case on their previous visit, as their host had made all too plain while rolling his eyes significantly from his plumply nubile young daughters to a truly impressive breech-loading shotgun above the fireplace.

And grey-bearded Pop had been right. Much too young and innocent for a pair of bitter-eyed vengeance hunters. But that had been two and a half years ago and the daughters, as they'd realized on checking in, had matured. Man! How they'd matured!

The little singer was disappointed to see them quit the cantina a short time later with the excuse that they had long miles to travel tomorrow to reach the next village and the hour was already late, whereas in reality they had dates. Tentative and potentially dangerous dates at that point of time, but dates none the less.

They were heading for Hogan's along Pierro Pass's one half-way-decent street when the shuffling bum approached, looking to cadge a dime for 'coffee'. They didn't even slow until realizing that beneath the hair and grime was an American. They turned and came back. Pleasure called but business would always take precedence.

'Got a buck for an old sojer, boys?' quavered the wreck.

Freeman sniffed at the stink and waved a five spot under the man's nose.

'The Mexes are too scared to talk to us, Pops. But an old Yanky soldier like yourself isn't scared of anything, right?'

'Er . . . right, I guess.'

'Jaeger,' Cobb said flatly. 'What do you know about Kyle Jaeger, soldier?'

Suddenly the drunk looked sober and scared.

'Damnit, I just want a drink, not a quick funeral — '

He broke off as Freeman stuffed the five in his breast-pocket, then produced a ten.

'You keep talking and I'll keep producing these, Pops. We know this is his bailiwick, so, where does Jaeger hang his hat?'

When the man eventually began to talk there was no silencing him. Freeman was down fifty dollars by the time they moved on but figured they'd gotten off cheap. No, the bum wasn't totally sure what base Jaeger called home but did know he spent a great deal of time roaming the province and holing up on the top-valley ranch of Don Patricio; the general belief was that Jaeger and Patricio were about as close as a tyrant and his hatchet-man could be, he speculated, looking nervously over one shoulder.

'What's he do?' Cobb asked bluntly. 'Apart from kill, that is. We know how he rates at that.'

The little wreck shrugged and spread his hands.

'Them Jaegermen will do anything — beat up on the Dons' rivals and enemies, shoot people who buck the system — in the back and in the dark, mostly. *Rurales* won't touch 'em — they're all in together now, them gunners and the so-called *Nuevos Rurales*. You see, we're too far away from the capital and the Federale headquarters for the powers that be to carry any real weight here, so — '

'We know all that,' said Freeman. 'About Jaeger?'

The bum stroked grey-stubbled cheeks.

'Seems to me he shuns the limelight, and that ain't easy for a feller his size. But he's always there, you can sense it.

Them hardcases what ride for him are scared cross-eyed of him, and who'd blame 'em?' He nodded emphatically. 'Uh-huh, you could say rightly it'd be hard to pin nothin' on Jaeger personal, but I reckon you could wager your last sawbuck that if anyone's beat up, shot, disappears or has his *jacal* burnt to the ground on account he won't work on the farmlands for peanuts, Jaeger is the man behind it.'

Satisfied they were making some sort of progress, the partners headed off to see if the Hogan girls were waiting for them, as planned.

They were unaware of the dark eyes of Captain Melgosa watching from his chair on the darkened porch of the cantina.

The good captain returned inside and crossed to the bar for a night-cap, where he made the acquaintance of the little singer. They got to chatting and he eventually escorted her to her quarters. She considered him quite romantic if a little ancient. But the evening didn't end well after Margarita realized that all Melgosa was interested in was what she knew about her 'friends', Freeman and Cobb.

4

Spur of Hate

Jaeger entered Pierro Pass in the dark of the night. The moon was a feeble slice in the sky and the stars were too few to shed much light. He walked with the reins of his horse looped over one arm. He passed a drunk holding a heated argument with a yellow hound over the salvage rights to a can of garbage. The drunk turned and called something after the big dark figure but he kept walking, his face shadowed beneath his hat and the yellow glow of a street-light falling briefly across heavy shoulders.

He passed a solitary woman on a shadowy corner — the last patient *puta* in Pierro Pass's lonesome night, hoping against hope that some last lonesome Joe might happen by, some loser hungry for the solace of flesh.

The woman came to the edge of the walk and was shaping her lips to accost him when something held her, some primitive instinct for survival that all street women must possess naturally if they are to stay alive.

He shook his head and for just a moment reflected street-light bouncing from his shirtfront underlit his face and she stifled a gasp.

This one was seen in Pierro but rarely, and then mostly in the company of other gringos with guns and hatchet faces. She knew his name and it was not a name to be mentioned carelessly, for reasons she barely understood.

He trudged on, wearied not by the miles but by emotion. Whenever he'd come to Pierro since his return from the north it had been as Jaeger the shadowy power-broker who issued orders, then sat in plush salons conferring with rich and powerful men while his hellions carried out whatever orders he handed them.

Tonight that disciplined Jaeger was no place to be seen: in his place the lethal ghost of his hellion past — that slim-hipped and boyish butcher gripped by the thrill of the imminent kill.

He had reverted to type.

He knew it. It was a weakness he'd vowed never to succumb to again, yet nothing could stop him now. Of course he could justify his actions and make them appear logical. The reappearance of Freeman and Cobb was a direct and immediate threat, for he knew in every fibre that they were coming after him. But for the moment he had the edge, insofar as they had no idea where he was while he knew exactly where to find them in this place that he knew like the back of his hand.

Sure, he was raging and the old fire tingled his fingers. But even were he calm and considered, he knew he should not pass up this one chance to get them before they had one hope in hell of getting him.

Why wait for them maybe to close in

on him, when his lightning response right now could snuff out any threat they posed in the space of a heartbeat?

He touched gun butt and his fingers tingled. This was just one night, he told himself. Surely the new Jaeger could wear the old Jaeger's hat just for a few short hours when the stakes were so high and the odds slanted his way?

Damn right!

He moved steadily towards the plaza, knowing where they were, sleeping and unsuspecting beneath the old quarter-moon slyly peeking out from behind its cloud cover now.

Eagerness was overtaking him and his heart began to trot as was always the case when he was about to spill blood.

The village the night-comer walked comprised an outsize plaza fronted by markets, stores, cantinas and the new, rough-hewn premises of the *Nuevos Rurales*.

Spreading out from the plaza with no apparent design were a hundred scattered adobes and two hotels, beyond them on the south-western side, a shapeless sprawl of hovels and shacks comprising the slums that characterized just about every south-of-the-border town in these seasons of hardship and want.

The night-comer moved silently along walls pitted with bullet holes. Fallen plaster exposed naked adobe. A sneer rode Jaeger's mouth as, crossing the square, he sighted a sleeper, obviously American, draped across a battered porch with his face to the sky. Sonora was filled with gringo losers. He despised them even more than the Mexican poor. Yet they served a purpose. They reminded him what he could be if he wasn't Kyle Jaeger.

He tethered his horse under a cottonwood on a silent corner and strode on. He kept to the shadows until reaching the broad open space that had been the parade ground of an army depot in the early days.

Now the area was flanked on one side by the squat, high-roofed ugliness of the hotelkeeper's house and directly opposite a long brick-and-tile edifice with a long row of darkened windows under a garish sign reading: HOGAN'S HOTEL.

He halted, sniffing the air like a predator. This was almost certainly the closest he'd ever been to the two who'd humiliated him, damn nigh killed him several times, then hounded him clear out of the country.

Moving closer to the wide deep gallery that completely encircled the Hogan house, he brought a section of the hotel stables into view. A beautiful sorrel hung its drowsy head over the top railing. He licked his lips. Exactly the breed of high quality horseflesh those vengeance-hunters would run to!

Jaeger made no sound as he mounted the house gallery. A dark bulky shape hanging from the rafters in the corner turned out to be a side of beef draped in cheesecloth. Hogan's bedroom door stood open and loud snoring drifted out.

Too bad he had to wake the old son of a bitch. But there were ten rooms in the hotel and there was no way he was about to start in going from door to door and waking everybody in the place. This had to be quick, slick and error-free. So he must have room numbers.

Hogan's room lay in deep darkness. Jaeger paused just inside the door for a moment to allow his eyes to adjust to the gloom. The room was about twenty feet square. He'd stayed here once when Hogan was away visiting Grande Ronde with his daughters. He always took his daughters with him. The man had a morbid fear the girls might lose their innocence, in which case he would not be able to marry them off to some bloatedly rich old Mexican rancher and retire on his charity.

The floor was carpeted, muffling the sounds as he moved to the end of the big old four-poster. He reached down and shook the sleeping man's shoulder.

The moment hairy old Hogan jerked

awake a big hand clapped over his mouth. He blinked like a hoot-owl as he stared up at the face above him and went rigid when recognition hit.

He was a tough old bird who began to struggle and squirm. Jaeger smacked him hard across the head with the flat of his hand to send his false teeth flying across the room.

'Shut up, you old dumb-ass!' Jaeger's voice was a low hiss. 'I ain't about to harm you any, grandpa, just give me numbers. Nod if you understand.'

Hogan's head bobbed. He was rigid with terror.

'Room numbers,' Jaeger said. 'Cobb and Freeman's. And don't tell me they ain't here or I'll make your ass wish it had never been born.' He eased his hand away from the mouth. 'Talk!'

At a time like this, Hogan would have told the Devil where God lived.

'N . . . number nine . . . that's Freeman . . . and number ten — '

He stopped in mid-sentence as a light footfall sounded on the porch outside.

Beyond the curtained windows a dim shadow moved. Hogan jerked erect and Jaeger twisted his arm cruelly up his back.

'Who the frig is that?' the killer hissed.

'I don't know — I swear to God!'

Without a whisper of sound, big sixgun jutting from his fist, Jaeger eased towards the door to get an angle through the window. He immediately made out the towering silhouette of a man standing by the hanging side of beef. Something glinted in the figure's hand and the watcher realized he was cutting at the meat. The man turned his head a little and reflected moonlight briefly touched a shock of yellow hair.

Buck Cobb was a towhead!

The killer turned to the ghostly, staring shape in the bed and silently cocked the weapon.

'Don't make a sound,' he warned. 'Don't you even breathe.'

★ ★ ★

Tousled, pretty, and drowsy with sleep the girl awoke with a start. Her first thought was that her father had somehow gotten a whiff of deception and immorality in the pure night air and had arrived at Buck's room with his buffalo gun, frothing at the mouth.

She snapped up into a sitting position. The lamp was lit and she had to blink twice to realize it was not her father but Buck Cobb standing stripped to the waist and barefooted at the end of the bed testing the sharpness of a wicked-looking Bowie knife on the ball of a thumb.

He grinned. She thought he had the biggest and boldest grin she'd ever seen. Then she realized she was sitting up bird-naked, and grabbed for the covers.

'It's OK,' he said quietly. 'I ain't the shy type.'

'What . . . what on earth are you doing?' The younger of Hogan's two overprotected daughters was considered the most attractive girl in town,

84

blue-eyed, a full but trim figure and lips like overripe cherries — or so Cobb thought. Those lips hung open for a moment, then began forming querulous questions. Why was he up and wide awake at God alone knew what hour in the morning? What did he intend doing with that knife? And — had he changed that much since they'd first met over two years ago — changed from about the nicest boy she'd ever met into some kind of maniac?

He just chuckled tolerantly and brushed the window drape aside to stare across at the house.

'Same old country boy,' he reassured. He rubbed his flat belly then slung his gunbelt over one shoulder. 'Just got overtook by the hungries, is all. Couldn't help noticing that handsome side of prime steer over to the house earlier, Eva. Say, do you reckon you could get a fire going in that old stove while I go slice us a couple of steaks? We could have us a fine . . . '

'You want to cook steak at this time?'

He was heading barefoot for the door.

'Cut and cook now, jawbone later, blue-eyes. I'll be back before you know it.'

'But . . . '

That was as far as she got before he slipped through the door and closed it soundlessly behind him.

Crossing the wide yard under a weak moon Cobb was suddenly aware that this was the first time he'd come close to feeling relaxed since the night they got the word in Durant. True, there was the uncertainty of knowing whether they would pick up on the killer's trail again, but he was reassured by the fact that one or two folks here had hinted that Grande Ronde might prove a place worth visiting.

A huge steak breakfast, an early start and they could be walking the streets of Grande Ronde by darkdown.

But first things first.

He made no sound as he mounted the gallery at the corner. He paused, knife at the ready to listen. No snoring. From their earlier visit he recalled Old Man Hogan snored all night long. Shrugging, he fingered the cover cloth from the beef and began to cut. Ten feet away in the darkened room, Hogan held his breath tight in his bony-ribbed old chest as he watched Jaeger steal towards the door. His throat constricted as he clearly heard Cobb grunt as he paused in his cutting to take a fresh purchase on the carcass. Hogan opened his mouth but no sound came out. Jaeger paused to glance back with a warning glare. Hogan was terrified of the man but his fear that harm might befall his daughters gave him the courage he so desperately needed. Abruptly his throat unlocked.

'Cobb!' he croaked hoarsely. 'Watch out, boy!'

But for the warning shout Cobb might have been dead six times over. As it was he barely had time to slip behind the carcass and whip his gun from its holster before an apparition clutching a blazing six shooter erupted from Hogan's doorway.

Three bullets thudded into the side of beef causing it to twitch and swing on its overhead castors. It was the beef jolting into Cobb that caused his first shot to go wild. He could see Jaeger's eyes blazing as the man came lunging at him, realized he had but one chance. Dropping a powerful shoulder low, he drove it into the beef with every ounce of his strength behind it. The side slammed into Jaeger with sickening force, sending his sixgun one way and the man the other.

In his haste to get his gun working again Cobb overlooked the return swing of the meat. The carcass struck his right hand and arm and his .45 went flying. Cobb didn't miss a beat as he hurled his big body for the doorway where the killer had disappeared. Inside the room old Hogan was screaming and pelting pillows towards the second door which was swiftly closing behind Jaeger's back.

'There's a cutter in my drawer, Cobb!' the oldster roared but the Arizonan didn't even glance his way as he hurled himself through space to hit the door with a shuddering crash. It held and he reeled back with agony coursing through his upper arm. He regained balance instantly and set upon the locked door again, this time with big bare feet. Hinges weakened by the first onslaught, the door trembled then fell with a crash into a darkened hallway. He leapt it, hit the ground running and sped the length of the passageway to reach a small window where he glimpsed a tall figure vaulting a corral fence to be instantly swallowed by the gloom beyond.

In the yard, Cobb ran just as fast as any 240-pound horseman could.

He charged headlong into the first alley where something struck his upper left chest with a sharp stab of pain and clattered metallically to ground behind him.

He couldn't let the killer escape again.

The knife had come from above. He hadn't seen Jaeger atop the wall but he heard him land on the far side.

Slower now, with hot blood coursing down his torso, Cobb made it to the first cross-street where lights were beginning to appear in the windows. He groaned on glimpsing the running figure, an impossible fifty yards distant, swinging round a corner into the square. Jaeger had to have a horse there — of course the bastard would! He gave that fifty yards all he had left. But his only reward was the sight of dust rising against the sky and the dark centaur shape of a man astride a swift horse bolting headlong into the mouth of an alleyway that led to the shanty town, to vanish in an instant.

★   ★   ★

No shanty-towner had seen, heard or knew one solitary goddamned thing — or so they claimed.

Not even the temptation of a handful

of ten-dollar bills could persuade even one scrawny field hand, gaunt-cheeked woman or pot-bellied kid to admit they'd seen or even heard a man astride a huge blood horse roaring through the lean-tos, clapboards and tarpaper shacks.

'They're too freaking scared,' Cobb panted, shoving his money back into his Levis. 'Have you ever seen anyone so scared?'

'Scared and smart,' drawled Freeman, turning to lead his horse back towards the square. 'They know we'll be gone at first light. But Jaeger could well be back — next year or even tonight. That's what's scaring them.'

Cobb knew he was right even though that didn't make him feel one lick better. Jaeger was long gone.

By first light he could be twenty miles away in country he must now know like the back of his hand, likely with the gang he was said to run with. Or he might well be hidden and protected someplace by the rich and powerful whom people said were his friends. It seemed to the manhunters that this was very much Jaeger's land as they made their goodbyes at Hogan's at daybreak.

That they'd missed a rare opportunity there was no doubt, and they realized that comparing the task ahead with their chase years earlier simply didn't make good sense.

Then, Jaeger had been just a desperate killer on the run, looking for someplace to hide. This new Jaeger who'd come so close to killing Cobb was emerging as some kind of shadowy power linked with the rich and influential of the region which, if true, made him a far more formidable proposition.

Which posed the query: would that new Kyle Jaeger run from them again as he'd once done?

The cheering answer had to be no. And they kept reminding one another of that as they followed their hunches west under a sky white with heat.

The scattered fragments of information they'd gathered about their quarry suggested they direct their quest towards Grande Ronde and the Valley of the Dons.

5

Jaeger's Town

By the time a sleepless Freeman grew aware of a soft light showing in the east, he knew he'd had his fill of Pierro Pass. Jaeger was out there somewhere — God alone knew where — but they sure weren't about to come up with any leads on him here. He strode back to Hogan's to find Cobb had beaten him back. Was already saddling both horses in the peeled-pole corral. Eva and Estelle stood by watching and dabbing at their pretty eyes while their father paced up and down the house gallery giving a recounting of the night's episode to the small crowd that had assembled in the yard.

The Mexicans stared at Freeman with big round eyes as he went across to kiss the girls goodbye. Hogan came hobbling across as they mounted. He urged them to stay, yet it was plain he would be relieved to see their backs. They'd drawn Jaeger right to his doorstep, and for all his tough talk the windy old reprobate knew he would rather attract a Biblical plague of snakes to his doorstep than that one.

'What'd you do to them *Rurales*?' he asked curiously as the two mounted. Then he grinned. 'They came griping to me but I told them it was you who done the shooting. They went lookin' for you, but just rode by with their tails between their legs . . . '

'What say we ride and cut the jaw?' Cobb said impatiently.

'Suits me.' Freeman waved his fancy hat. '*Adios*, sweethearts! See you on the way back . . . maybe.'

The girls waved and they moved their horses into a trot. Looked like another hot one coming up.

The trail was long, dry and every bit as hot as predicted. Yet they made good time to noon at a place called Devil's

Rock, then swung up and rode out of the shade, the sudden sun striking like a hammerhead.

Several hours' riding later, the long grey smudge on the horizon slowly took on a more definable shape and grew longer, taller and higher through shimmering heatwaves until eventually assuming the majestic outline of the Big Bosque Mountains.

Cobb, never wrong about such things, calculated they would make Grande Ronde by sundown.

★   ★   ★

'There it lies,' Jose Santiago Espado announced with a catch in his voice and a dramatic sweep of the hand. 'Paradise on earth.' He paused for effect before adding bitterly. 'Or at least as it once was.'

Espado's young cousin, visiting the province for the first time, stared wide-eyed at the spectacle below and thought: For once Uncle Jose does not exaggerate. Paradise it must be.

The two Arizonans, the girl and the youthful kinsman with an ancient pistol thrust through the worn six-inch leather belt holding up his ragged charros, all leaned forward to take in more of the sprawling vistas on a day when the valley seemed to be putting on its finest face.

The group occupied a high granite look-out point on the western side of the horseshoe-shaped valley from which they could look down on to the slopes of the near valley side, where thickening stands of pine and juniper flourished. A slab of white stone projected half-way down, upon it an antlered stag standing motionless as though posing for a cattle-drench calendar.

The animal sensed something and was gone with a click of heels and the goodbye flash of a white tail.

Cousin Gallardo didn't even notice as his wondering gaze took in the meadow green of the rolling expanses of cattle-land fringed on the near side by luxurious beds of wild flowers, in the distance the red and white blobs of cattle grazed — above, a cascade spilling down a thousand feet over the distant opposite wall to feed the river.

The Rio Arriba tumbled down through twenty miles of high upland valley grazeland from its origins in the soaring immensity of timeless rock which formed the U of the mighty horseshoe shape of Saragoza Valley. It pinched in to a narrow neck again upon reaching the flatlands to the north, then spread out beyond where a thousand acres of intensely cultivated farmlands, storage barns and irrigation channels formed variegated patterns of green, gold and brown The ever diminishing east and west prongs of the horseshoe were barely visible beyond the farmlands until they finally disappeared altogether into the rolling plains country beyond, with Grande Ronde just a distant blur of colour beneath the canopy of smoke haze.

From the look-out one could barely

make out the high roofs and turrets of Don Patricio's headquarters sprawled upon the high southern reaches of the valley's cattle-lands, encircled to its rear by rearing cliffs and mighty trees.

Several miles closer stood the blinding-white hacienda, outbuildings, corrals and amateur bullring of Don Valdez. Only partially visible some distance further downslope, where the valley's walls sloped away gracefully until swallowed by farmlands and plains, stood the impressive if slightly less grandiose adobe castle of Don D'Palma, whom hard-hating Jose Santiago Espado hated more than God hates sin. But then, lean and hungry Espado hated them all. Every rich rancher, every money-lending Midas and foreclosing banker or captain of industry, all were high on his list of those guilty of the destruction of the old almost sublime rural way of life for which he'd fought — and mostly lost — virtually all his adult life.

Short but stocky of physique with a

mobile haunted face under a mat of greying black hair, no-longer-young Espado still looked the part of the wild-eyed rebel and hero of the poor even if his best days were behind him.

It was the unforeseen armistice and union of the dons which had driven the nails into this freedom fighter's coffin. Prior to that black day, with Patricio Valdez and D'Palma living like princes and fighting each other like mongrel dogs, his position as spokesman and advocate of the poor had been infinitely stronger. That turbulent situation had offered him the unique opportunity to play one *rico* against another. It also reduced the level of opposition whenever he organized his *peóns* to hold out for better conditions, or staged one of his by now almost forgotten protest marches on the streets and squares of Grande Ronde.

Gone were the days.

The peace pact between the aristocrats, which Espado fiercely believed to have been the handiwork of Don

Patricio's enforcer, Jaeger, had in turn seen the old activist confined to his adobe in town by the *Nuevos* who finally shut down all his rebellious activities.

Following several protest breakouts and indiscretions, the rebel and his family had been bundled off to the sheep land where they were now obliged to seek permission from the law even to visit Grande Ronde.

So he sat and drank and railed endlessly against inequality, and only occasionally stirred himself to visit the look-out and see with his own sad eyes how much richer the rich were getting, and how his 'shirtless ones' were faring under the tyranny of the overseers.

His daughter always insisted he should never come here, that their miserable little sheep town was infinitely better for him, and consequently for them all. At times he would agree yet still he came. He might well keep coming here until either he was called to Heaven or rose up in bloody rage at the head of a ragged army for one last defiant attempt to destroy the great *hacienderos* — but much more likely to go to his death.

'I have never seen such riches, Jose.' The cousin sounded impressed yet bitter underneath, for he was cut from the same cloth as Espado. 'Nor such poverty as I have seen in the town. Why is it so?'

But all Espado could do was extend arms wide with tears in his eyes while the angry young man fingered his gun and the splendid girl looked bored to death. Juanita, daughter of Jose, had viewed this scene too often.

Now Jose began again to speak nostalgically of the good old days; when he'd dwelt in the valley and when the dons had hated one another's guts, yet were forced to take care of their *peóns* who were often the foot soldiers in the ongoing conflict between the landowners.

He explained to Gallardo how the dons made their peace and immediately found themselves powerful enough to force every last campesino, Indian or ragged Mexican off his little plot of farmlands earth. Consequently, with the support of the newly formed *Nuevos Rurales* — another Jaeger improvisation — they were in a position to force the half-starving former lot-holders to return to work for them as virtual slaves.

'But the great days shall return . . . ' Juanita heard her father say, and stifled a yawn.

As sensually statuesque as an Aztec princess with waist-length black hair and perfect high-cheekboned face, the rebel's daughter was not unfeeling, just weary. Weary of the endless talking, the planning, the plots that were never realized and the 'great day of rebellion' she heard so much of yet knew would never come.

Juanita turned her sleek head as the young man approached.

'He will talk himself to death one day, your father,' he said with a smile.

'You do not talk much, do you, Gallardo?'

'Talk is for women.'

'Why talk when one can die young, eh?'

'You mock me, Juanita. But I would rather die young for a reason than end up an old man with no reason to be still alive.'

'Everybody must accept that from the day the dons united, our struggle was all over, Gallardo. Suddenly they had the numbers, the hired riders and the leaders — '

'And Gringo Jaeger!' he cut in angrily.

'*Sí*. Jaeger again! Jaeger is the reality here, cousin. Those huge gringos with their guns and their cruelty towards us are as jaguars toying with new-born lambs — '

'Look!' Espado interrupted. He was pointing up valley where a gleaming coach and four flanked by eight armed outriders suddenly appeared to take a graceful curve in the downhill trail.

'Patricio!' Espado mouthed bitterly. 'See him in his pride,' he sneered. 'That *hombre* is a weakling, yet he now lives like a king. I have seen him almost in tears when he knew I had bested him. Now if I crossed before him in the square he would order his reinsman to drive over me. How could such changes come to pass?'

No one responded as they followed the progress of the equipage and escort all the way down to reach at last the lowland sprawl of the farmlands.

From the distance it appeared as though the patchwork quilt of the farmlands itself was actually moving until it was realized that the illusion was created by the vast number of workers at their labour.

The splendid entourage was eventually swallowed in the dust rising off tilled fields.

The old rebel, suddenly appearing shrunken, turned and led them back to the ponies.

'Crummy whiskey.'

'What'd you expect? Kentucky bourbon?'

'How's your beer?'

'Warm.'

'What else?'

Cobb removed his Stetson and used it to bang the dust off his knees. He perched it on the back of his head and closed one eye to study his partner standing below his position on the plankwalk by the hitchrail.

'Know something, Freeman?'

'What?'

'You usen't always to be so grouchy.'

'Maybe it's this lousy whiskey.'

'I'm serious. You started to sour as soon as we knew Jaeger'd given us the slip again. We spend a day and a half getting here and all you've done is gripe instead of getting busy. You want to run him down or not?'

Freeman's steely eyes flared. At odd times since their reunion in Durant it had been almost like the old days when the firm of Freeman and Cobb might impulsively conceive a big beef deal, do business with cattlemen, rustle up a trail crew then drive maybe 2000 head 500 miles to a railroad, make or lose a fortune on the deal, and do all of it without a hitch and with high spirits.

But times like this the wedge that had been driven between them by the tragedy of Salvation Creek seemed wide as ever.

A caustic retort went begging as Freeman realized that the other might well have a point. And had to ask himself, what in hell was he doing down here in a remote quarter of up-country Sonora being harassed by hellions and viewed with deep suspicion by just about everyone in sight — if he didn't still truly believe in their crusade? And yet he did. More strongly than ever, if anything.

So, Pierro Pass had been bad. So, get over it!

He straightened from the hitchrail

and stared into his glass. He shot the contents into a trash can, followed by the glass. He looked up.

'OK, what are we waiting for? Let's go find out what the law can do to assist us.'

Cobb just grinned amiably as they started off to take a closer look at Grande Ronde.

It was a sizeable and sprawling plains town with a muddy river running through it and the dramatic backdrop of the Big Bosques looming to the south.

Like most such towns in the region it was built around a wide and dusty square filled with people, vendors, bare-legged kids and lean and hawk-faced men sucking thin cigarillos beneath the shade of huge sombreros.

Several substantial buildings distinguished Grande Ronde from most other places of its size. Virtually all of these were in some way linked with the real rulers here, the dons. Communally they owned a glass-fronted bank, several huge shipping stores and warehouses and sweatshops where those too young, old or infirm to labour in the fields could sew, cook, fashion, carve, hammer or hew at tasks related to the dons and all they produced.

There was a scattering of Americans on the streets, mostly cold-eyed gunmen and loners, exiles, mystery men or outlaws who could never return home.

The sudden appearance of two strange gringos alerted the hard-faced 'lawmen' watching from the shade of the porch overhang.

As the *Rurales* noticed them, they noticed the *Rurales*.

They noted that the heavily armed men in uniform slouching, sitting or half-sleeping on the long, low front porch of the long, low brick and adobe building with barred windows sported the same insignia as the so-called *Nuevos Rurales* they'd encountered further east.

As had been the case back at Pierro

Pass, the NR personnel didn't look like regular lawmen; they more closely resembled cantina sweepings who'd been stuffed into uniforms and told to go act official.

They approached the jailhouse and picked out one of the uniforms standing in a doorway who seemed to have some authority.

They approached and introduced themselves.

He was a lieutenant in the *Nuevos Rurales*, the man supplied coldly. What did they want? And if they were here to cause trouble, as most gringos did, they would regret it.

It wasn't a promising start. But they persevered. First Freeman produced cigars of such quality that the officer simply could not resist. Then Cobb got the man to loosen up some by first casually discussing the weather, the local beer and the high price of good horse-feed these days.

Eventually they were invited inside where they saw about a dozen cells, most of them occupied.

'Enemies of progress,' the man sneered. 'We try to persuade them to accept the changes. Some do, some do not. Why, even tomorrow, one such troublemaker is to face the firing squad. Perhaps the gringos would like to witness this event? You could be the guests of Lieutenant Fernando.'

The two traded glances. The lieutenant was trying to intimidate. He was letting them know he played the game hard in case they were here to raise trouble. Cobb left it to Freeman to convince the fellow that they were simply cattle-dealers from the States on vacation who'd heard about the beauty of Ocotillo Province and had chosen to visit.

The lieutenant seemed to swallow most of this. Indeed Freeman seemed to be doing quite well until he mentioned the name 'Jaeger'.

'Jaeger?' All trace of affability left the *Rurale*'s face. 'What is he to you?'

Freeman had plainly touched a

nerve. He attempted to shrug it off but in smart time they found themselves ushered outside where the *Nuevos* stared hard while Fernando offered a little advice.

'I suggest you do not tarry long in Grande Ronde, gringos,' he warned. 'It could be dangerous to do so . . . as a matter of fact I can guarantee that such would prove the case. Do I make myself clear?'

They gave Fernando the hard eye. He took a backwards step but he still had the nerve to rest a shaky hand on the holstered pistol at his side. 'Vete!'

'Well, that went well,' Freeman muttered when they were safely out of earshot. His tone was ironic.

'Reckon we've made a new friend,' Cobb half-grinned. He glanced back over his shoulder. 'Well, at least we know.'

'Know what?'

'That mebbe them stories we heard about Jaeger and his standing out here might be true. That'd explain Fernando turning sour when we dropped the name.'

'If that's the case, I need a drink.'

They made their way to the nearest cantina and ordered beers. Freeman no longer trusted Grande Ronde whiskey. Or Grande Ronde itself for that matter.

While still at the bar they chanced to fall into conversation with a stove-up *vaquero* who proved to be no friend of the law, the dons, or a man he'd never met but hated anyway, Kyle Jaeger. It was from this man they first heard the name, Jose Santiago Espado.

★ ★ ★

Don Patricio sniffed. The stuffy little room in the padre's house in back of the church was windowless. It smelled of Indian, he thought. Although fierce sunlight blazed down outside, it would have been totally dark here but for the glow of a single tallow candle. The padre had received him here before. Claimed the room's windowless hush was conducive to reflection and meaningful conversation. Even the smallest room in the don's place up-valley was at least four times this size. And there was no Indian smell there. Not at the hacienda nor anywhere on the ranch.

The man who regarded himself as leader of the Saragoza Valley triumvirate was tall, lean and immaculately attired in broadcloth and satins. He gave a courtly bow when the portly figure in a floor-length soutane strode in vigorously, some of his diffidence disappearing when Padre Carrizo opened the varnished doors of a wooden cupboard and took out bottle and goblets.

Whether Patricio was top dog of the three dons or not was open to discussion. But nobody disputed the fact that he could imbibe more wine, spirits or pulque than Valdez and D'Palma put together.

The amenities attended to they sat opposite one another at the table. Padre Carrizo, chubby-cheeked and fringed

114

around his bald dome, smiled amiably.

'And how may I help you, Don Patricio?'

'I have a problem, Padre.'

'Living itself can be a problem.'

Hardly in the mood for platitudes, Patricio took a swig of red wine and dabbed fastidiously at his lips with a lace-trimmed kerchief. For a brutal slavemaster, the don often appeared remarkably delicate.

'I believe it is time for a festival, Padre.'

'I'm afraid there's nothing on the church calendar in the near future . . . '

'I'm aware of that.' Patricio forced a smile. 'But I'm quite sure you can drag out some forgotten saint or martyr and tell your congregation it's time the poor wretch had a little recognition.'

'Well . . . '

'You see Padre, I've discussed this with Valdez and D'Palma and we all agree that we could all do with a touch of veneer.'

'Veneer?

'Gloss, polish — something to make us shine. Although this has been our most productive season ever, there is also an unpleasant side. The *peóns* are eternally complaining about such matters as pay and conditions, the rich and the poor. So we decided that what we need is a festival, one sponsored and conducted by Holy Mother Church, of course, the purpose of which will be to demonstrate how much we care for the poor and want them to be happy.'

'Er, you might consider improving their lot, Don Patricio?'

'What a quaint notion,' Patricio said dismissively, rising and collecting his fashionable hat. 'Well then, Padre, I trust I can leave this matter in your capable hands?'

'As ever, Don Patricio, as ever.'

When the don had gone the good padre felt tempted to pour himself a stiff one. He resisted and crossed the paved yard to the church to pray instead. It seemed that just about all he could ever do for the poor these days was pray. But he never gave up the hope that once, just once before being called to his reward, he might get to do something more practical to save both the souls and bodies of the dons' wretched slaves.

6

Rebel Country

Tierney and Crites forded the high mountain stream and pushed lathered horses on downslope, the sun glinting from crossed cartridge belts and the metal hook that substituted for Crites' left hand.

Jaeger's topkick and his gun lackey knew this sector of the Big Bosques well. This dated back to the time three years back when a wounded Jaeger had holed up here when a pair of Arizonan cattle-drovers were hunting him like wolfhounds on the scent of a honey-bear.

As events turned out back then, Freeman and Cobb had lost the scent a hundred miles south and had never made it up to the Big Bosque region before heading home. But unaware that the pair had quit on him, a desperate Jaeger had by then made his decision to quit Mexico and take ship north.

He left all but Tierney behind him in Sonora. By the time he returned a year on he was a much-changed man with far loftier ambitions than just running off cows or sticking up banks. As a result of his change in ambition and direction, Jaeger had since grown powerful and influential in remote Ocotillo Province, collecting Crites and most of the old bunch about him as he began to surge up the ladder of success.

Tierney was reflecting on such matters as he kicked his grey mare ahead of his *segundo* to enter the narrow draw. The blocky killer with the hatchet face rode relaxed in the saddle and far easier in his mind now that Kyle had bounced back in the wake of the Pierro Pass affair.

Claiming to be the one who knew Jaeger best, Tierney had at first been both startled and baffled by the other's decision to go after Freeman and Cobb, one-out, when at the time he could have mustered twenty men to back his play — more if required.

Jaeger had eventually explained his actions, revealing that the realization that his old persecutors had come back to Sonora had thrown him initially. It was the timing of the pair's re-emergence that had jolted Jaeger most, for their arrival in the province came at the worst possible time for his plans.

Tierney immediately understood. He was the only Jaegerman who fully comprehended the scope of the leader's grandiose plans eventually to take over from the dons and see himself installed as virtual king of the province.

Jaeger had already set the date of his takeover. It would be at the 'Festival of the Dons' in Grande Ronde. The festival and his dark plans for it was to be the realization of the vision that had come to him during that winter in the California diggings where, in-between freezing his teeth out and smashing up troublesome Cousin Jack miners on behalf of the camp bosses, a perceptive, hungry Jaeger had observed at first hand the stirring example of a bunch of woolly-headed Welsh miners literally taking over a mining empire by craft, guile and cold-blooded murder.

'The only law you must obey in such matters, Kyle, me boyo,' so the leader of the Welshmen had boasted, deep in his celebratory cups after the coup, 'is the 'possession is nine points of the law', law.' A huge triumphant smile. 'Backed up always by the generous bribe and, if that fails, Brother Colt, of course.'

Upon his return to Mexico he'd realized that compliance with the Ocotillo law would be essential for the lasting success of his overthrow. In this case events played into his hands when government in the far-distant capital decommissioned the drunken rabble which passed for lawmen in the province and Jaeger, acting with the full support of the dons whom by now he had eating out of his hand, had shown himself to be the only man capable of identifying and assembling the hand-picked bunch of 'volunteers' necessary for the task. When the dons supported him, he was given the task, which was how a bunch of American and Mexican hellions got to be duly sworn in as peacekeepers under the *Nuevos Rurales*.

Every single *Nuevo Rurale* was beholden to Jaeger, not the law. This would prove vital come The Day.

And it had been Jaeger's passionate determination that nothing would be allowed to interfere with his ambitions that had seen him go after Freeman and Cobb — whom he still believed would be now lying cold in their graves, but for a lousy side of beef.

Maybe so. But that was past.

Pierro Pass had been a mistake. You were allowed one.

Jaeger had insisted they would take care of the Arizonans but possibly not until after the takeover, and that was good enough for his loyal *segundo*. He'd also been promised he would play the major role on the night of blood which was currently known as the Festival of the Dons.

The festival had also been Jaeger's idea. Tierney didn't know how he came up with them. The gunman grinned as they picked their way along a dusty trail for the sheep town. Today's assignment fell under the heading of 'setting the stage and lining up the cast'.

Tierney shifted his weight in the saddle as he glimpsed the conical roofs of a scatter of mud huts up ahead.

'Ho, greasers!' he bawled as they rode into the little sheep town. 'Git out here afore we come in after you, Espado!'

Within minutes they were all standing before them, the sun-darkened men, the slatternly women, the big-eyed kids and the girl who had the gunmen staring today, just as she always did.

Tierney forced himself to focus upon the man they'd come to see. People claimed Espado was all washed up, just a shadow of the rabble-rousing troublemaker he'd been in the fields, the work-sheds and out on the ranges of the valley before Jaeger got the dons to merge. One of the first positive actions of the triumvirate had been to kick Espado's sorry ass out of Grande Ronde all the way up here to live with the sheep where he belonged.

Tierney had never believed Espado was all through. But he did believe he could be conned into playing an important role in the fiesta, if handled right.

'*Quiénes?*' the man demanded, knowing full well who they were.

'Shut up and listen. Yesterday, you bums were sighted up on the cliffs over the valley. What were you doing?'

'Admiring the view, *señor.*'

'Who the hell are you?' he demanded of the young stranger.

'Gallardo, cousin of Juanita.'

'Well, shut up — cousin.' He returned his attention to Espado. 'We figure you were spying again. What do you say to that, Mex?'

Espado remained poker-faced. 'We do no harm — '

'Button up, greaser! We don't trust you and your dog-pack, never did. I'm here to remind you that you're only here by the good grace of the don who can kick your sorry asses out of the province any time he wants. Things look like being pretty busy hereabouts leading up to the big festival, and I'm here to let you sheepers know Grande Ronde is off limits to the whole bunch of you until after the big night. It's to honour the dons and we don't want any of you rabble-rousing scum making speeches and getting folks stirred up. So hear me good. You'll stay put here, but if any one of you might be thinking of getting up to your old tricks we'll come down on you like a goddamn avalanche. You can believe that if you never believe anything else. Hear me?'

A silence. Then, 'Is that all Jaeger had to say?' Espado asked quietly.

'No more tricks or spying or running off at the mouth?'

'You have my word, Señor Tierney.'

It was quiet after the gunmen left.

Scuffling his toe in the dust, Espado was aware of the eyes upon him. They were shocked by his meekness and he did nothing to relieve them as he walked away to his *jacal* where his bottle waited.

Only his daughter followed. She folded her arms and studied him suspiciously where he sat on his stoop nursing his brandy.

'*Que?*' he grunted.

'You do not deceive me, old man.'

'What deceive? What foolishness do you talk?'

'The others think you are the coward. But Tierney does not.'

'You speak in riddles. Be plain or be silent.'

'The way he spoke to you about not attending the fiesta was just as I would speak to my stubborn papa if I *wanted* him to do something.'

She smiled. 'For you are stubborn and proud and would simply have to do the opposite — as always!'

The man's gaze brightened as he took a swig. He made no reply but his daughter knew he would defy Tierney. In that moment she felt both fearful but deeply stirred. She was after all a rebel's daughter.

★   ★   ★

'The toast is to our guest. *Señors*, be upstanding.'

Three men attired in the typical finery and accoutrements of the Spanish aristocracy came to their feet and lifted glasses high.

'Señor Kyle!' they said in unison, and drank.

Jaeger nodded gravely. Impressive in broadcloth jacket, string tie and with no big guns showing, he was proving the perfect guest of the dons, just as he had proved to be the inspired unifier, visionary and staunch lieutenant of the *ricos* throughout a vital period of resurgence in their history.

The occasion tonight had been organized by the dons specifically to express their gratitude to the man who'd first shown them how and why they should unite, then demonstrated how to subjugate the town, the workers and even the very law itself until all these elements were working for the triumvirate and not against them.

So who deserved recognition more?

The atmosphere relaxed following the toasts and the tequila, whiskey and rum flowed freely.

'You do me a great honour,' Jaeger told his hosts, nursing his whiskey while they all drank and beamed. He paused then added: 'I feared that certain recent rumours might have troubled you some. About me, I mean.'

'You mean, about Pierro Pass?' Patricio said, and Jaeger nodded. 'Well, of course we did hear something . . . '

'All lies,' Jaeger insisted. 'I wasn't even here at the time.'

They seemed to believe his denial but he realized they'd heard the whispers when Valdez said curiously:

'Is it true that you had some connection with these gringo *pistoleros* whom our *Rurales* are watching closely at this very moment, *amigo* Kyle?'

'We're old enemies,' he admitted. 'They're *renegados*, outlaws, Mexican-hating scum. But they can't hurt me and I won't let them hurt you. So just don't you fret about Freeman and Cobb, *señors*. Leave them to me.' His smile was reassuring. 'You've told me often you admire the way I clean up messy situations and tidy loose ends. Sooner or later our *Rurales* or myself will take care of that pair, rest assured.'

'Did they buy that?' queried Tierney as they shared a quiet drink later.

Jaeger leaned his broad back against the bar.

'Bought it, liked it, Wolf. They're so used to me solving everything they'd believe it if I told them the sun wouldn't rise tomorrow.'

'You know, I gotta tell you something, Kyle. When you came back from

California with them big ideas, I wasn't sure you could do it. I could see too many hitches, too much that could go wrong. But watching you there tonight with the dons eating out of the palm of your hand, I wondered what the hell I've been worrying about.'

'I was the redeemer they never realized they needed,' Jaeger said with one of his rare smiles. 'I got rid of their rustlers, smashed Espado and his rebellion, finally got the three of them to kiss and make up. Hell! I even stopped the railroad coming in, didn't I?'

Tierney had to admit this was so. When the Hermosillo government decided to extend the railroad westward as far as Ocotillo Province, the dons were horrified. They ruled like feudal barons here and rightly feared that the railroad would bring changes and enlightenment, and they welcomed neither. A series of attacks on railroad installations and the murder of track-layers and timber-cutters had seen the distant government recently announce the cancellation of the Ocotillo Line — another debt his 'employers' owed Jaeger.

But as always he'd operated behind the scenes. Everyone would learn who and what he really was soon enough.

'One for the road, Kyle?'

'Got business.'

'I got Wichita, Crites and Parlee waiting to escort you wherever you want to go, Kyle.'

'You fret more about Freeman and Cobb than I do, mister.'

'Well, you're calling the shots, Kyle.' Tierney grinned. 'Er . . . you going to watch it?'

Turing to leave, Jaeger paused with a frown. 'Watch what?'

'The execution.'

'Hell no! You know how bloodshed turns my guts.'

Both laughed. That was really a good one.

★   ★   ★

131

Three sides of the jailhouse yard and horse-corral were blocked off from the first light by the towering bulk of Castillo's hay barn, but the timid early beams flooded across the battered fourth wall, the horse stables, highlighting the heads and shoulders of the silent people gathered in the morning chill, waiting for it to happen.

They didn't have to wait long.

Suddenly light and sound spilled from the jailhouse and all heads turned to see the burly *Rurales* hustling the prisoner round the stables' corner, and half-pull, half-push the shabby figure towards the steel ring set in the scarred wall.

Standing together behind the crowd, Freeman and Cobb traded silent glances. Each was thinking the same thought, it could have been an atmosphere much like this when a bunch of rustlers prepared to snuff out five young lives.

The prisoner was silent, staring at the faces before him as they lashed him to the ring while the three *Rurale* riflemen moved into position across by the barn. With his rags and beard he resembled a gaunt Jesus about to die — for what?

The Arizonans didn't realize he was a trouble-maker until the *teniente* appeared to read out gruffly the charges which included 'attempted insurrection and overthrow of authority'.

At those words, the prisoner drew himself up and began shouting.

'Slavery is a sin! *Amigos*, defend your brothers in the valley as Espado once exhorted you. Do not — '

The *teniente*'s right arm rose and fell and the roar of the volley overpowered the dull sound of the roped body striking the hard caliche of the area abutting the horse-stables' wall where the dark stain swiftly spread.

★ ★ ★

Freeman glanced up from his frijoles. 'Did you smell Jaeger's hand in that execution?'

133

'Sure thing.' Cobb paused as he watched a gunman peer through the window then move on. 'They're watching us right enough, but there's no sign of Jaeger. What do you figure?'

'This is his town; we're next door to sure of that now. He plainly has the number, yet he's not making any move. Do you figure we might have scared him off at Pierro?'

'Do you?'

'Not for a moment. So, that could suggest he's waiting for an appropriate time to deal with us.'

Cobb busied his hand with tobacco and papers. He was frowning.

'Weird, ain't it? We bust our humps coming after this bastard, nearly get killed at Riata then come nigh to killing him at Pierro Pass. Yet now when we've finally run him to ground we find we can't finish it off on account we don't rightly know where to look. And even if we did, he's got enough pistoleers, friends in high places and even the law in his pocket to wipe out a small army.

What do they call a situation like that?'

'Ironical.'

'Yeah, iran — what you said.' Cobb lit up and drew deep. 'Anyways, I sure as shooting don't feel like sitting around waiting on that sonuva. I'm going horsebacking.'

Freeman frowned. 'Where?'

Cobb rose and dropped coins on the table, his head barely clearing the ceiling. 'There's a hell of a lot going on hereabouts that I'd like to look at and get a line on. If we gotta bide our time on Jaeger we might as well take a look-see around. Mebbe we might hunt up that feller we heard about, Espado.'

'I knew it,' Freeman said, taking down his hat and fitting it to his head at just the exact angle. 'As soon as they told us about that man, I knew the 'under-dog's friend' — Buck Cobb — would have to take the bait.'

'Does that mean you ain't coming?'

Freeman half-grinned. 'Did I say that?'

* * *

The two rode from town a short time later. On the post-office steps, Crites gestured for two of his men loading at the hitchrail to follow. But the hardcases just shook their heads. They wanted nothing to do with the Arizonans who'd once scared Jaeger out of New Mexico and eventually Sonora.

Crites cussed and scratched his neck with his hook, but didn't insist. Deep down he didn't blame them. The only man he knew who might challenge those Arizonans was Jaeger himself. But Kyle was busy with other matters today. Major matters.

* * *

From a distance the tiny sheep town studded the smooth brown hills like mounds of dung. They rode in and Cobb whistled through his teeth.

A man poked his head out of his *jacal.* '*Si?*'

136

'Freeman and Cobb to see Señor Espado.'

'We're friendlies,' Cobb added when the fellow blinked uncertainly.

A shaggy head appeared from a hut and growled. 'I am Jose Santiago Espado. *Quién es?*' He rubbed his eyes and glared. 'More stinking valley *pistoleros?*'

'Reassure the man,' Cobb said, swinging down. 'I'll water the horses yonder.'

Freeman walked off and Cobb took the sweating mounts across to an adobe trough, where kids began to gather round, big-eyeing the rugged gringo and the long-legged mount. Usually good with kids, Cobb paid them no attention. That was because he'd sighted the girl.

She was tall and slender with smooth olive skin, her body already curving into the lush ripeness of Spanish womanhood. She crossed to the trough unhesitatingly, where she folded her arms and studied him curiously.

'Howdy do,' he said, tipping his hat.

She nodded gravely in response.

'You are the gringo *pistoleros* who fought with Jaeger at Pierro Pass?'

That was his second surprise, the first being her beauty in this anything-but-beautiful town. He got her talking and she revealed how the whole region had heard of that gun battle by this; she'd merely sized him up as one of the 'two tall gringo gunmen' described, and taken an educated guess.

They chatted easily together for a time then went across to Espado's *jacal* where Cobb found Freeman considering a surprise invitation.

'I was telling the *señor* about your interest in conditions in the valley,' he said, 'and he's offered to take us to see for ourselves. What do you think?'

'Bit risky for you, ain't it, *señor*?' Cobb asked Espado. 'Didn't we hear you're banned over there?'

'The farmlands are dangerous. But if you are afraid . . . '

'What do you say, dude?' Cobb grunted.

Freeman didn't reply. He'd just gotten a clear look at the old fire-eater's daughter.

'*Madre de Dios!*'

'Ain't she though?' Cobb grinned.

'If you go, father,' Juanita said to her father, 'then I shall also go to keep you out of trouble.'

'Well,' Freeman said, 'if she goes we all go. You have any argument with that, Buck?'

The girl surveyed Cobb with those grave Spanish eyes.

'I go,' she said simply and Cobb just raised his hands and dropped them.

'Well,' he said, 'I guess that settles that.'

7

Raging Gun

This was high up in the Big Bosques where the winds blew restlessly across the mighty loft of the mountain curve that enclosed the highest, richest and least accessible of the three cattle ranches comprising Saragoza Valley.

It had taken two hours to climb just a mile or two from the plateau half-way up the valley where they'd been forced to leave the horses.

By the time they reached the look-out spot, a rare slab of ancient stone without any surrounding vegetation to block the view, Freeman needed a shot from his hip flask while Cobb took out his field glasses.

The glittering white hacienda of Don Patricio dominated the emerald-green rangeland a mile from where they stood sucking in air and swabbing perspiration.

It was as impressive a sight as a man could wish to see with its white-painted wooden fences, outbuildings, servants' quarters and stockyards. Yet neither man was much interested, and Cobb quickly had his glasses trained on the second ranch house on the slope beyond and somewhat below Don Patricio's headquarters.

It too was a handsome building, yet drew no more than a cursory glance. The big Arizonan was adjusting the settings on his glasses to bring into sharper focus the men who could be seen working or loafing close to the house.

There were five or six of them in sight. After a minute, Cobb grunted and passed the glasses silently to Freeman. He fiddled with the screws a moment then slowly panned across the yards, came back again to the rear entranceway where three men stood smoking in the shade of an oak.

All were heavily armed and dangerous-looking; they looked nothing like ranch hands and everything like hardcases!

'So it's true' he said slowly, lowering the glasses. 'This is where he hangs his hat . . . and he and the don would be safe from an army up here.'

'Looks like.'

'How many do you calculate we've seen since we arrived?'

'Seven or eight. There's likely more going by the number of saddle horses in the yards.'

Freeman leaned against a rock shoulder and took out his cheroots.

'So let's look at what we've got. Plainly Jaeger's in as thick with Patricio as we've been led to believe. In turn that means he's tight with the other two. So . . . that means between us and him there could be as many as a dozen gunmen backed up by *vaqueros* . . . take your own guess how many. And each time we've sighted him he's been riding with a pack that we'd have to be loco to take on.'

Cobb nodded soberly.

'Seems to me he must've had a rush of blood to the head when he came after us in Pierro. He was lucky to get out of that, but you can't say the man ain't lots smarter than when we were after him before. He's pulled in his horns, made use of the setup he's fashioned for himself . . . now he can just sit back safe and wait for us to make the next mistake . . . Hey! Speak of the devil! Lookit!'

Freeman snapped the glasses to his eyes as the towering figure came striding across the hacienda's rear gallery. The sun struck Jaeger as he made for the yards with men falling in behind. The silent pair above watched with fingers flicking at their sides as horses were cut out, saddled and led from the yard. Just the way Jaeger threw himself across his horse without fitting foot to stirrup showed a man at the peak of his powers, secure in his arrogance, unassailable.

Within minutes the party was taking

the down-valley trail, Jaeger riding easy in the saddle and flanked by men on every side.

And all they could do was stand and watch.

They'd never expected this. They stared at one another in silence, then shrugged.

After three long years, they'd tracked the killer to his lair, yet suddenly he seemed further out of their reach than ever.

Freeman was relieved when Cobb suggested they go visit Espado to see what that old rebel might come up with. For once the team of Freeman and Cobb appeared to be stymied.

*   *   *

The fishermen were getting riled. It was raging hot along the willow banks of the Rio Arriba with the glare coming off the water punishing to the eyes and nothing in the basket after four boring hours of plying their lines.

'How come we got posted here today anyway?' Benteen growled, fiddling with fly and hook. He turned to stare moodily up at the cliff trail that wound down off the western arm of the enclosing mountains to cross the river a short distance downstream. 'Why does anyone get posted here for that matter? It ain't like nobody ever dast come down here any more.'

Two heads nodded in agreement. It was a long time since do-gooders from town, or thieves looking to steal something from the farmlands a mile downstream, had been last intercepted here by Jaeger's men. They'd learned that lesson to their cost.

'I reckon this postin's more punishment than anything,' big Rand growled. 'They told Kyle we was seen dogging them Arizonans round town last night after Wolf warned us to let 'em be.'

'Beats me why Jaeger don't unleash us on them two,' Turlock chimed in, scowling at his line trailing limply in the backwater. 'Anybody'd think he was skeered of 'em. Judas Priest, they're just a pair of gunnies. Two of them against all of us and the *Nuevos*? You'd think they was the Texas Rangers.'

'Fast gunnies,' corrected Benteen, rising to cast. 'Had to be to nail McCrow and Littleman like they done.'

'All the more reason for us to go after the sons of bitches!' Turlock argued. 'Goddamnit, they damn nigh hounded Jaeger into his grave before, and now . . . ' The man broke off abruptly, swinging his bullet head towards the trail. 'What was that?'

They listened, and stared. Hoofbeats!

The trio radiated eagerness for trouble in the way they shot their rods aside and started up the slope of the bank. The trail was gained just as the strange bunch of riders came swinging into sight around the willow-hung S-bend upstream.

The riders appeared odd due to the fact that they all wore big straw peasant sombreros and shapeless serapes.

The party reined in sharply as the

146

trio, swaggering now, strode towards them.

'What the hell — ?' Rand began, breaking off when he could clearly glimpse the lead rider's face. 'Espado! What the hell's name are you doing here, you stinking old . . .'

His voice tapered off as a sombrero was fingered back to reveal the striking features of the old renegade's daughter. '*Señorita*,' he fawned, with a sickening smile. Then, 'Judas Priest!' he gasped and he went backwards two long steps upon finding himself staring at the uncovered features of Luke Freeman and Buck Cobb. The colour drained from leathery cheeks. 'What in the blue hell . . . ?'

'Forget it!'

Cobb's warning cracked loud as Benteen shot a glance over his shoulder in the direction of their rifles stacked against a willow trunk. The pale-faced hardcase cursed, but stayed put.

'What's this all about, Espado?' Turlock was the senior gunhand here and very conscious of his authority. 'This trail is off limits and nobody knows it better than these sneaking sheep-stinkers.'

His big head nodded. 'As for you two gun-tippers — '

'You want we should turn back, Jose?' Freeman spoke over him.

'Is a free country, no?' Espado was drawing courage from the company. He leaned forward and grinned down at Turlock. 'No, I think we go on. Run and tell big bad Jaeger what we do, why don't you, little gringo lapdog?'

Everything happened at once.

Lunging forward with a curse, Turlock seized Espado by the leg and dragged him to ground with a crash. The gunman sensed movement in back of him and behind him and whirled to see Freeman hit ground and come at him.

Turlock let go of Espado and charged.

Freeman straightened the gunman with a perfect straight left then threw a right that never landed as Benteen crash-tackled him from behind. The two hit ground and rolled. Rand was rushing up to join in the affray when Cobb beat him to it.

Cobb's driving haymaker caught the side of a fast-rising Benteen's head with a sound like an axe biting into wet wood. The man went down again as though poleaxed. But Cobb hit ground himself a split second later with his head ringing like a gong. Dazedly the big Arizonan realized Rand had whipped off a big high-heeled cowboy boot and slammed it against the side of his head.

Next moment Freeman and Turlock were going at it hard, Freeman boxing like he was still on the team in college, Turlock hurling haymakers like grenades.

Cobb recovered quickly as he sprang to his feet. Rand was struggling to jerk off his second boot when Cobb reached him and pistoned a knee into his guts. The hardcase fell in a heap and Cobb

deliberately stomped on his unpro-
tected foot as he headed for Turlock,
the only one of the trio now left
standing.

Juanita was the only spectator evi-
dently not enjoying the spectacle of the
brutal free-for-all. Instead she appeared
bored and superior, like a mother
watching the children rough-housing.
But Cousin Gallardo shouted encour-
agement to the Arizonans while a
still-mounted Espado was vigorously
throwing phantom punches and holler-
ing:

'Get 'em, big boys! Ponch the left
and the right!'

Cobb was observing no rules of
encounter as he reached out and tapped
the brawling Turlock on the shoulder.
When the man spun round Freeman
instantly took full advantage and
collected the hard man with as fancy a
straight right as the boxing tutors in St
Paul ever saw.

The brawler went down in a heap
and it was over.

'You didn't warn us this trail was sentried,' panted Freeman, taking down his cattleman's lariat from his horse. 'You said you'd just bring us down here to see a thing or two.'

'Is not always, *amigo*.' Espado was still highly excited. It was too long since he'd witnessed the full-heated crunch and thud of an honest-to-God brawl.

His eyebrows shot up quizzically as Freeman and Cobb began slinging rope around their still-dazed opponents. 'So . . . what you do now?' His face lit up with sudden expectation. 'We lynch?'

'*Papá!*' the girl chided, and the old rebel grinned to show he was only joking.

'We'll truss and gag them while we go see what we came to see.' Cobb was panting as he dragged Turlock through the dust like a sack of potatoes towards the willow.

'But . . . but, this could be danger-ous, *amigos*. When Jaeger and the dons hear of this they will — '

'They'll hear whether we quit now or

go on in,' declared Freeman, dragging two bloody-faced men at once by the collars. 'We can only hang once.'

'Only hang once!' Espado chuckled. 'You gringos plenty funny. But — '

'No buts.' Cobb was emphatic as he finished trussing his man to the tree. He turned to assist Freeman. 'You start a thing, you see it through. Right?'

'Right,' affirmed the other.

The slowly recovering hardcases said nothing at all. But in time, they would.

★   ★   ★

It was like looking through the gates of hell!

Anonymous in huge straw sombreros and shapeless ponchos, Freeman and Cobb stared from the window of the derelict barn at a spectacle that might once have been familiar in the deep South pre-war, but not since.

Slavery had been abolished in the States but not here.

The farmlands, which sprawled for

miles across the foot of the lush valley from their position had appeared pretty and bustling from a distance, but from up close proved a nightmare.

Adjacent to the big old barn standing on the west rim of the tilled fields by the river, lay a vast cotton field where scores of men, women and children were picking under the eyes of mounted riders toting guns and whips.

A lash cracked and they saw an emaciated figure go down. The picker rose hurriedly and resumed his work. As far as the eye could see there was more of the same, women loading heavy baskets of produce on to a Conestoga; bare-chested men smothered in blood slicing up beef carcasses in the shadow of a slaughterhouse; wretched human beings crawling around in the heat like ants. And everywhere the mounted overseers urging them on, whips glinting snake-like in the hot sun.

'Maybe the *Americanos* have seen enough to realize that what we have told them is true?' Espado said from beneath his floppy hatbrim.

A grim-jawed Cobb glanced at Freeman, nodded. For one day, they felt they'd seen and done more than enough.

★   ★   ★

Kyle Jaeger could be murderous in his silent rages. Whenever these moods overcame him even flinty-eyed desperadoes ducked for cover. But when he just sat staring, or paced up and down with jaw muscles rippling and black eyes darting and flickering like a snake's, a man never knew whether it was going to blow over or blow up.

The powerful figure stalked from one end of the gallery to the other, hands locked behind his back, as oblivious to the spectacular sunset as he was to the edgy gunmen watching him from a prudent distance.

He eventually halted on the front steps of the large rambling house which had been Don Patricio's hacienda before he built his glittering white palace a quarter-mile distant atop the hill. The lovely old building comfortably accommodated all the Jaegermen in remote privacy and security. It had been a gift from Don Patricio to his 'great *compañero*' Jaeger for bringing 'peace' to his valley.

Don Patricio and the killer went back quite aways.

* * *

It had been during his desperate flight from two remorseless manhunters almost three years ago that a haggard, hurting Jaeger had temporarily given the Arizonans the slip in the southern foothills of the big Bosque range to thread his solitary way through the myriad of valleys and canyons to stumble eventually upon the Valley of the Dons.

They were grim days of uncertainty for the dons as they feuded with

Grande Ronde, with the rustler threatening their fine herds, and most fiercely with one another.

That day, as fortune would have it, when the ragged gringo killer and *renegado* suddenly came riding out of the tall timber down by the farmlands, Patricio was unwisely returning to the valley by a little-used back road following an altercation with the so-called rebels of Grande Ronde, with just two escorts. When a mob of workers hoeing corn realized just who it was who'd blundered by, they broke ranks and angrily surrounded his coach before it could get through.

Jaeger reined in and watched the ugly situation develop. His lip curled at sight of the ragged *peóns*, a breed he despised, but his interest quickened as he began to note the quality of the besieged Don's horseflesh and the fine coach; the glitter of his jewellery.

This was a desperate hellion hungry for refuge, reward, anything he could get before a pair of gunpacking hell-riders picked up his scent again and ran him down with not even a faithful Tierney at his side to stand by him now.

On impulse he spurred straight into the ragged mob, cutting left and right with a chopping gunbarrel before the hairy-faced leader whipped out a rusted pistol. With less compunction than you'd kill a rat, Jaeger blasted the loser to death — and spent that night and several others following under the roof of Patricio's former hacienda as the honoured guest of a grateful don as a consequence.

Simple gratitude on the part of one man and raging envy and avarice in the other, was quickly replaced by something else, at least on the don's part.

The *rico* immediately recognized in his accidental saviour the total ruthlessness he knew to be in himself, even if they were men of vastly different breeds. While Patricio was an aristo, born to wealth and privilege, and Jaeger a mad-dog killer, there was an empathy between them that stemmed from each man's ambition and selfishness coupled with a total indifference to human life or suffering. Each intuitively detected the similarity in the other; so, instead of Patricio rewarding the renegade with a swift kiss-off just as soon as he was safe, or Jaeger maybe taking advantage of his momentary position to rob and kill — they took a long appraising look at one another and decided they both could do far better by cultivating the other.

Overnight Jaeger became Patricio's confidante and numero uno bodyguard. The killer, with an eye to the future, noted every aspect of Patricio's situation and background while reaping rich rewards which might well have continued had he been able to stay on. But one bright morning while out buffalo-hunting on the plains north of Grande Ronde with his new *patrón*, Jaeger, still not fully recovered from his earlier brush with death, had glanced up to sight two distant figures astride all-too familiar horses on the far horizon.

He fled.

They came after him as before but failed to run him down. Jaeger had made an emergency arrangement with Tierney prior to fleeing north. As a consequence when he eventually reached the southern seaport of Mazal-tan, more dead than alive due to a reinfected gunshot wound, he found his faithful *segundo* patiently waiting — the windjammer unfurling her canvas ready to sail.

The good ship *Santa Aldara* was five miles out to sea with a following wind by the time two trail-gaunt gringo horsemen dusted into the port, where they proceeded to tie on a monumental booze-up before heading back for Arizona defeated after six months on a killer's trail.

Sea air and a leisurely two weeks leaning against a ship's rail saw Jaeger regain his old vigour, and the pair made it safely all the way on to the California diggings where for a time they scraped a precarious living by robbing muddy little diggers of their pathetic pokes.

Eventually they secured jobs as personal bodyguards to a consortium of rapacious mining kings and thus met up with a bunch of single-minded Welshmen whose cunning, cleverness and celebration of the 'possession is nine points of the law' philosophy changed Kyle Jaeger's murderous life for ever.

★   ★   ★

Jaeger inhaled deeply.

He stood with hands locked behind him, powerful legs wide apart, his large head angled forward as he stared over the heads of a dozen silent henchmen who didn't want to stay but lacked the nerve to leave.

His reflections had calmed him some, yet he still looked strange enough to guarantee that nobody dared shuffle off.

It was a time since they'd seen him as hard as this. Indeed, ever since consolidating his position with the dons and setting up here with his gun-crew to live like a prosperous cattle rancher himself, the killer had seemed to rein in his once-famous temper and only occasionally bawled someone out or belted a man unconscious for some stupidity or other.

Some believed Jaeger had not been himself ever since the day at Zacario Mesa when Struther Cady brought news of the first Freeman-Cobb sighting.

There wasn't a gunman who didn't believe the leader hadn't lost control that night — heading back to Pierro Pass alone as he'd done. Only Tierney thought otherwise. That was because Tierney understood that it had mainly been the perceived threat to Jaeger's overall grand plan that had driven him to take that seemingly reckless decision, not spite or revenge. He reckoned Jaeger had only wanted to cancel out a potential threat to his ambitions that night, not just simply count coup on enemies like some crazy gunkid.

Of course tonight's alarms aroused by the incident along the Rio Arriba had to be regarded as serious. No outsiders were ever permitted into the farmlands. When dangermen such as Freeman, Cobb and Jose Espado had been involved in an intrusion there it couldn't help but set warning bells clanging. But if Jaeger was so damn riled, why didn't he do something about it instead of just staring and brooding like a big old buffalo bull?

The gunmen began muttering amongst themselves as daylight drained away. At last Tierney dropped down off the corral fence and strolled across to the gallery with feigned casualness, red thatch competing with the sun's last crimson minutes.

Jaeger fixed him with a black-eyed stare. He didn't speak.

'You're making the boys jittery, Kyle.'

'Who gives a damn?'

162

'Bad time to unsettle men . . . right when we're working up to the big one.'

'Who asked you, mister?' Jaeger's voice was gunbarrel hard. But almost instantly he swore under his breath and tugged out a cigar, knowing he must unwind or else run the risk of doing something foolish: going off half-cocked. 'Of course you're right, damnit. But I planned all along to just shove that pair to one side until after the big night, then go after them with all hands.'

He bit the end off the weed and spat it away viciously.

'But I gotta face it. That plan's beginning to look too damned risky now . . . them horning in and sniffing around like they've been doing. They could blow it all!'

'They gotta go, Kyle.' Tierney's voice was flat, unemotional. He could talk murder as casually as another might order groceries. He gestured. 'Plenty of the boys eager, of course. Some of 'em kind of feel you've been holding them

163

back where the Arizonans is concerned. There's any number of talented guns keen to put that pair under the grass for you, y'know?'

Jaeger sucked smoke into his lungs then tilted his head back to blow it high.

'They know where to find them?'

'Sure. We've been keeping tabs.'

'OK. Do it.'

8

Bullet Talk

'What's that?'

'What's what?

'Something in the ceiling. Can't you hear it?'

'Owls.'

'What do you mean — owls? This is — or was — a goddamn hotel. Owls are outdoor creatures.'

'Owls will be owls, as my pappy used to say.'

That shut Freeman up. He knew he could survive roosting in the spooky turret room of a tumbledown hotel — despite having a comfortable rooming-house bed undisturbed waiting for him not fifty yards distant — if circumstances required. But he couldn't handle anything remotely connected to Pappy Cobb on a night like this.

Silence settled again.

Despite Freeman's physical discomfort it had been his decision to camp away from their lodgings for a few nights. They'd done so the previous night, now again. Cobb hadn't objected. The reality of life in Grande Ronde was getting through to them; they had their quarry, but Jaeger had the numbers.

It was painfully hard just to stand back and wait for an opportunity after running their fox to ground at last. But they were manhunters first, avengers second. They hadn't come this far just to buck the odds and get to fill nameless graves while Jaeger survived.

Their moment would come; they must wait for it.

Yet even apart from the Jaeger factor, the atmosphere in Grande Ronde had been tense and uneasy from the outset. This was due not only to the presence of the Jaegermen, there were also the hostile *Rurales* to concern them, along with the everyday citizens who largely gave them a wide berth on account of all the rumours circulating about them.

Their precautions that had seemed a sound idea on the first night, appeared doubly so tonight in the wake of events out at the valley. They regretted tangling with the Jaegermen earlier. They'd had no intention of raising the dust there, had been simply killing time waiting for Jaeger to make his first big mistake when agreeing to accompany Espado to the valley.

They were hard men to shock but could still feel the outrage experienced at what they'd seen at the farmlands. That was as bad as it could get, yet in no way diverted them from their main purpose. They simply could not afford to get sidetracked by anything at this time. They were like men who'd ground something into themselves so obsessively there was no letting go.

Get Jaeger! was still the name of the game.

Freeman was dozing lightly on his rough bench-bed when he heard Cobb

167

hiss sharply. He sat up muttering. Moonlight angled through the cracked window-pane. A silent Cobb pointed down and Freeman rose to see lights flickering on in the rooming-house windows which had been dark before.

They hauled sixguns and watched.

Shadows moved past windows, faint voices drifted on the night air. Then the front door of the roomer opened and a man toting a rifle appeared. He stood a moment looking both ways before making his way out to the kerb. He was shortly followed by another, and they glimpsed shadows in the building's yard in back.

Cobb and Freeman traded glances.

'That rooster in the plaid shirt is Turlock,' Cobb whispered.

'And the geezer looking up and down the street — he was one of the bunch that braced us that first day we showed.'

'Jaegermen!'

'You said it.'

'You know, cowboy, I don't know about you, but I've had a bellyful of this. Five will get you ten that that bunch snaked into our roomer looking to blow us out of our beds. We've been holding back here while waiting our chance at Jaeger. But we could get ourselves killed if we just sit back and wait for them to jump us next time when we mightn't be so sharp. Right?'

'Keerect.' Cobb was already heading for the rickety loft ladder.

Freeman followed, checking his guns.

Turlock was standing in the centre of the side street as the two reached ground level. Others were drifting across, talking, spitting and cussing with rifles in hand. They acted like they owned the damn place, which maybe was the case.

'Looking for someone?'

Cobb's voice coming from the darkened doorway carried clearly. Figures started and swung their weapons in the direction of the hotel.

'Who's there? Come out or we shoot!'

'You were looking to shoot anyway,

you dry-gulching sons of bitches!'

'Turlock!' a narrow-gutted gunman said in a hoarse whisper. 'I know that voice, man. It's them. It's the fraggin' Arizonans!'

Turlock flinched. He backed up a pace. Others in the group weren't so jittery; they hadn't been dished up along the Rio Arriba as he had been. Rifle hammers cocked and faces glared at the doorway, where Freeman looked at Cobb who stared right back. That look said it all.

It was action time.

Still without a word but with hands clutching four revolvers, the two strode from the doorway and headed directly across the street towards the trouble.

The effect was dramatic. From belligerent aggressors one moment, in the next Turlock and his bunch were looking like awkward bully boys who'd just had the rug jerked out from under them. By contrast Freeman and Cobb looked exactly like the two who'd gotten the better of Jaeger in Pierro

Pass, and for a handful of seconds the hellions didn't seem to know whether to fight or run.

That was all the time it took for them to be reached. Without pause, without a word, Freeman backhanded an ugly towhead across the mouth with his gunbarrel to send him spinning headlong into the gutter. Now a scrawny runt cursed and tried to bring his rifle up but proved way too slow. Cobb crunched him with a pile-driving shoulder then kicked both legs from under him to drop him like a bag of dirt.

It went swiftly from there and there were five hellions down before the hard-breathing victors heard the swift stutter of running feet.

They turned sharply.

'Hola!' hollered a voice thick with mescal and wrath. 'Do not move or we shoot.'

The Grande Ronde *Nuevos Rurales* had arrived!

'Butt out or you're meat, *homrecito*!'

Cobb retorted and once again the Arizonans moved aggressively towards the threat. Their blood was up and they were ready to party.

For a tense moment the *Rurale* trio stood their ground. But bluff was more potent than bullets here tonight, and abruptly the pock-faced officer back-pedalled several paces before gesturing to his men to lower their weapons.

Instantly, like the well-trained team they were, Freeman and Cobb moved sideways to command the centre of the street from where they could cover both groups.

'Some coincidence you *Nuevos* just showing up here in the middle of the night!' Freeman's tone was sarcastic. 'It couldn't be that you were waiting close by to see how your pards here made out against us, could it?'

'We are the law!' the officer said. 'And you gringos are breaking the law.'

'And you're a yellow dog posing as law!' Cobb shot back, and the situation was looking dangerous again when it happened.

A man came striding down the street, small, upright, uniformed and familiar.

'Host with vinegar! What is the meaning of this? What happens here?'

Freeman and Cobb stared, then grinned. Captain Melgosa of the *Federales* could not have been a more welcome sight. They might not know the little man well enough to call him a friend, but they were to discover he was no friend or admirer of the *Nuevos Rurales* either.

★   ★   ★

The captain sipped his rooming-house coffee, smiling at the landlady who stood awaiting his reaction.

'*Fantastico!*' he lied, and the good lady blushed with pleasure and waddled from the room in her exotically tie-dyed bathrobe to see to the tortillas.

Instantly the *Federale* fell sober again as he studied the two big men seated

173

opposite. 'I could have you taken into custody for assault and resisting arrest. I hope you understand that?'

'*Mi Capitán,*' Cobb replied amiably, 'we're in your debt. We trust you and we sure don't doubt you've got men available to back your play, like you say you have. But if you tried anything on us — you knowing we're with the law and not against it — we'd just have to mash you, I guess.'

'Mash?' the little man said. '*No comprendo.*'

'OK, OK, take it easy,' Freeman interjected with a warning frown at Cobb. 'As the man says, we owe you, Captain. But all we were doing was protecting ourselves. And judging by the way you bawled out the *Nuevos* and the guntoters, I reckon you know that. So, now we got that out of the way, why don't you tell us what brings you back, and how come you seem so jittery.'

It was true. Melgosa appeared drawn and tense, unable to relax. He sat staring from one to the other for a long moment as though coming to a decision about something. At last he sighed and leaned back in his rooming-house chair. He appeared to loosen up as he began to speak.

First thing he revealed was that he had been intensely busy since they'd last met. And, yes, he was extremely tense tonight, but with good reason.

The Arizonans sat in silence for the time it took Melgosa to explain how his investigations had led him to the belief that 'something huge and possibly sinister' was awaiting Grande Ronde.

He based this conclusion on many factors. High on that list was his sudden realization that the dons and their 'gringo gunmen' were bending or breaking every law in the book, with blatant slavery being perpetrated openly in the farmlands, a major crime even in Mexico. He was also convinced that the *Nuevos Rurales* were but a sham and possibly, even probably, in cahoots with the dons and their power élite.

This led the captain to the conclusion that events were rushing towards a climax for Grande Ronde. He conceded he might be unduly alarmed but they could tell that he genuinely believed in what he was saying. How, when or where this anticipated climax might erupt he could not speculate, he conceded. Yet his every officer's instinct clamoured that his intuition was not letting him down. He noted that citizens seemed wary and tense; there were strange movements of men, unexplained midnight meetings both here and at other places he'd observed.

Perhaps what disturbed him most was the kind of overheated excitement surrounding the upcoming 'Fiesta of the Dons'. This set his teeth on edge, for the dons, although dominant and in full control, were universally unpopular, causing him to be suspicious of this enthusiasm for the upcoming celebrations on the part of the very people they oppressed.

'So,' he concluded, looking more

relaxed for having unburdened himself. 'I have been frank with you, now you must be frank with me. What of your activities, *señors?* I have heard alarming rumours of your behaviour since we last spoke. Tonight, I'm quite certain that my appearance forestalled what was plainly shaping up as a highly serious situation, possibly a fatal one. I must insist it's high time we were open and honest with each other, *compañeros.* No?'

'No' was right.

They wanted to confide in Captain Melgosa but knew they could not. They were here to avenge a great crime. No genuine ranking officer of the *Federales* could condone that, while for their part nothing would divert Freeman and Cobb from their sworn mission.

They parted on distant terms.

★   ★   ★

The padre played his part in the forthcoming event. Although all too well aware that the Grande Ronde man in the street either disliked the dons at best, or at worst regarded them as the Evil Trinity, he used his pulpit as a platform from which to deliver an evening address calculated to encourage peace, harmony — and a full attendance tomorrow.

His motives were the best.

He was agonizingly aware of the inhuman conditions of the farmlands, had watched the dons grow bloated and arrogant through power and profit ever since the unification of the strong had resulted in the enslavement of the weak.

The congregation resisted their pastor, at first. Many were actual work-deadened drones from the farmlands themselves while others present had friends and kinfolk suffering out there.

There was also a voluble and volatile section of his flock present who would string up Patricio, Valdez and D'Palma from the nearest lamppost rather than celebrate their status. These were members of the once strong rebel movement which he feared might be preparing for trouble tomorrow if they thought they'd have one chance in a hundred of achieving anything.

But when it was all boiled down the hotheads probably knew there would be no upheavals. They must know, as did the padre, that there were far more lily-livers in town than fighters or idealists, which should guarantee that tomorrow's festival would prove a brilliant affair to brighten dull lives — with no violence — so why not attend?

'God knows we need something to cheer us up,' as one silver-haired old lady was heard saying with a sigh later. 'Of course we'll all be there, Padre.'

Satisfied he'd succeeded in his intention the good father locked up the church afterwards and retired to his little private prayer room to get down on his knees and beg forgiveness for being such a contemptible hypocrite.

At times in the secret realm of his

conscience, the man of God believed the best thing that could ever befall Grande Ronde would be if the Saviour were to grab all three dons by their scruffs and take them to heaven or the other place, and leave the poor and the worshipful to live out their simple and uneventful lives in peace, and, of course, holy observance.

* * *

That night, all over Grande Ronde, posters and decorations were going up. Some citizens would be busy with preparations until dawn. It was not the first time the dons had organized a tribute to themselves, and poor *campesinos*, Indians and those of pure Spanish blood alike took a kind of perverted pleasure at the prospect of debasing themselves before their oppressors yet again while at the same time praying to Saints Francis and Peter that all three might be struck down with yellow fever and the black

180

pox before next day's sunset.

The mood changed abruptly at a sudden clatter of hoofs and all paused in their chores to see a swarm of Jaegermen and *vaqueros* streaming into the *placita* on splendid horses. The riders circled all the way around before eventually coming to a halt before the temporary official dais which was in its final stages of construction in the north-west corner of the *placita* before the sturdy stone façade of the council supply store.

Some shivered as a familiar figure leapt lightly from saddle to platform and fingered back his hat to reveal the face of Jaeger himself.

Many blessed themselves, others spat curses. But prayers and cursers alike soon got on with their tasks, reminded afresh of what an important day tomorrow must be when this feared figure himself appeared publicly with his full gun force instead of lurking in the background as he mostly did.

Jaeger moved to the back of the dais

and spread his arms wide.

The killer was feeling expansive tonight. Behind him now, the endless planning, scheming and kowtowing to the dons. Ahead lay the hope, the action and the blinding uncertainty of the final hours.

Some of his men kept watch from their saddles while others joined him before the dais.

'The dons will be seated here,' he announced loudly for the benefit of the bystanders. 'Directly behind them, the six men I nominated — forming a solid line of defence in case some madman tries anything. You men know who you are and what your duties will be?'

Heads nodded.

'The alcalde will speak first, followed by the padre then the Chief of Rurales,' he went on. 'The speeches and tributes might take half an hour. The dons will respond, and after that — the real fun begins.'

Nearby workers didn't detect the irony in those final words. There was so much they didn't know, such as what was destined to prove the climax of tomorrow's 'celebrations'. Or the fact that the real instigator of the Festival of the Dons had not been the dons, but Kyle Jaeger himself.

A barricade of gunmen now ensured that nobody got close enough to overhear anything more that was said, as Jaeger and Tierney dropped to ground at the rear between the platform and the utility store.

Standing there out of sight of all but his own, Jaeger torched a cigar and flicked the dead match to land in the shadows beneath the platform.

'Right there,' he said. 'Five feet in, six feet from either side. X marks the spot for the dynamite package. You got that straight and clear?'

'Right, Kyle. I'll take care of it personal. That's the only way we can be sure it'll be done right. Where'll you be?'

'Well away, you can make book on that. Now remember, you touch off the fuse at eight on the stroke at the height of the riot. Then you bang on the planking on your way out to give our boys plenty of time to jump clear of the dais.'

Tierney grinned broadly as he envisaged the grisly climax to the Festival of the Dons. The desperadoes could easily have been just a couple of self-satisfied dirt farmers contemplating a record harvest, so easy and relaxed did they appear from a distance.

'It's took a long trail one way or another, Kyle, but it's gonna be worth it . . . ' The redheaded gunman frowned. 'Er, can we be sure there'll be a riot to cover us? By eight, I mean?'

'Depend on Espado. He'd swim a sea of blood to get here. That sawn-off greaser won't be able to resist a rare chance to show the world he still ain't afraid to cuss out the dons over everything from their expired title-deeds to the way they operate the farmlands as a slave plantation. But even if the runt turns shy, I've got a dozen *vaqueros* from the valley primed to start in punching rebel heads and kicking groins, coming on eight. Everybody'll be so geared-up by then that the ruckus will explode at first sign of trouble — who touched it off don't hardly count. In the middle of that ruckus, bang! Nobody'll know what happened until we tell 'em it was the greasers . . . '

Tierney broke off and scowled as a thought intruded. 'Where do you reckon they'll be when all hell busts loose, Kyle? You know what I mean?'

'We'll all be ready for them when the time comes. They fancy themselves as hard men but they've shown by the way they've yellowed out of coming after me here that they know I've got the edge. Well, tomorrow night right after the big bang, when the whole fraggin' square's in an uproar, every man Jack of us are going after Freeman and Cobb and there'll be no place they can run. And you can wager those two will get the blame for the explosion as well — after they're dead.'

He held up two fingers, eyes bright with savagery. 'First — the dons. Second — Freeman and Cobb. That's the playbill for this here festival and nothing is gonna change it.'

'And third — Don Jaeger,' Tierney chuckled. 'King of friggin' North-west Sonora!'

And dark laughter came again.

★ ★ ★

Don Patricio carried his brandy snifter along the west-wing corridor as he made his way towards the library. It was his favourite room, smelling of oiled oak and fine leather, books he seldom read and masculinity.

Women weren't welcome in the West Room; a nobleman needed some sanctuary. Mostly when he visited this room Patricio was in a relaxed mood which he pandered to here with good brandy, fine cigars and a wander round his paintings and sculptures, none of which he really admired for they had been chosen specifically to impress. He liked to bring his fellow dons here on occasions when he took delight in displaying his knowledge and appreciation of fine art, when in truth about the only example of the written word he truly appreciated was to be found on the title-deed that identified him as exclusive owner of 12,000 acres of prime upper-valley land. The deeds to South Valley had been invalidated by time-expiry years ago, as had similar worthless documents in the possession of Dons Valdez and D'Palma.

He set down his glass, took keys from the pocket of his silken lounging-jacket and opened a wall safe from which he withdrew a bundle of official-looking documents bound loosely together with pink ribbon.

To Patricio's twisted mind, the virtually worthless papers were a constant reaffirmation of his strength, leadership and ability to keep 'civilization' at bay in this remote backwater.

The capital would like nothing better than to revoke the old grants, kick the patriarchs out of the valley and bring that hated alien ideology, 'democracy', to Saragoza Valley.

How unfortunate for the mandarins of government in Hermosilo that they lacked the resources, the will and the daring to be able ever to make more than token gestures of imposing their authority here. And how fortunate for the dons.

The dons were Ocotillo's only authority. In recent times the trio, through Jaeger, had expanded and corrupted the *Nuevos Rurales* to such an extent that should Hermosilo ever attempt true reformation here the decadent 'lawmen' would oppose them side by side with the dons and the Jaegermen.

Patricio smiled as he moved to a huge plate-glass window and stared downslope to his left where the old hacienda stood with all lights burning tonight. Jaeger would be down there, sleepless but in total command, calmly preparing yet again to further the cause of the dons and cement their power.

Gratitude and admiration were rare emotions to this man. But he felt both towards Kyle Jaeger, and his attitude hadn't been any different from that day they'd first met under violent circumstances along the east trail not ten miles from where he now stood.

When the wounded Jaeger had appeared from nowhere to save Don Patricio's precious life from the mob it had been the beginning of a strange but potent friendship.

Jaeger was as impressive a man as the don had ever met. That day when they met the outlaw was in deep trouble after having been pursued all the way from New Mexico by gringo avengers, had to have one of their slugs gouged out of his side, and was eventually forced to take flight again when rumours had Freeman and Cobb circling the valley like vultures. Yet the man's strength and intelligence had shone through in a unique way, so much so that before the killer quit the valley the uncharacteristically grateful Don made him promise that if he ever made it back to Sonora he was to come look him up.

Gratitude had nothing to do with the don's invitation. He'd scented in the outlaw the kind of unique blend of ability, leadership and loyalty that he'd long been searching for in his besieged life amongst his valley enemies.

Jaeger had eventually returned to justify every high expectation the don had harboured. Had proved the perfect *segundo*, organizer, enforcer and yes, even peacemaker. He'd brought peace between the dons and, once they had been united, had shown them the way to command absolute power, leading to the brutal yet outstandingly successful enslavement of the working poor.

'I toast you, *amigo* Jaeger,' the slightly tipsy Patricio said aloud, raising his glass. Then he settled back in a huge leather chair and allowed his mind to wander luxuriously over a long and ever more successful future stretching into the decades ahead.

He had less than twenty-four hours to live.

9

The Gathering Storm

Freeman drawled, 'Your five and up five, *amigo*.'

'You bluff again, *señor*.'

'It'll cost you money to find out.'

The little Mexican scratched his head and suddenly, unexpectedly, threw down his cards.

'Is impossible,' he protested. 'I play well when I am drunk, when half-asleep. Even I play well when my pretty wife tickles my neck and begs me to carry her to bed. But tonight I am the big fool who cannot play even when the cards are fine. Why is it so?'

A circle of cantina late-nighters stared at the player in silence. Every drinker, player and yawning bar-girl knew the answer. It was not the player who was at fault but the night itself.

There was something in the very air, in the way an old hound-dog might awake suddenly and begin barking when there was nothing to bark at. In the little mud *jacals* weary mothers sat up pacifying babes who refused to sleep for no reason. Men wandered the streets alone or in groups, not for the company or the beauty of the night, but for the self-same reason that the canny card-player couldn't seem to tell a joker from a lowly deuce. Something was abroad and nobody seemed able to give it a name, but at least Buck Cobb took a shot at it.

'It's something that's called sleep,' he stated sarcastically, reaching for his hat. 'It's what smart folks do when they need it, but dumb ones would rather set up to all hours finding reasons not to do it, then start in griping when they give themselves the jitters. Mostly poker-players, I'm talking about.'

Freeman ignored the barb. As relaxed and unruffled at two in the morning as he'd been at sundown, he shuffled a deck, puffed on a cigar, began dealing himself a hand of solitaire.

'Well, you always were the sensible one, Arizona.' He glanced at the clock. 'Early to bed and early to rise, like always, eh?'

Some sniggered. Others covered up their mouths, as the giant *Americano*, usually genial and easy-going, scowled about him as though aware that he was just as wound up as anyone else, despite his protestations.

In truth this strange mood affected most of Grande Ronde tonight. A large number of those present at the cantina had been occupied throughout the day preparing for the fiesta, yet scarce any of them had left for bed. Right across the town it was the same. Restless citizens wandered the dimly lit plaza, cigarette-smoking *Nuevos Rurales* lounged on the jailhouse porch; even the padre had been sighted mooching around telling his wooden beads a short time back.

Every man sensed the reason for this

strange mood yet none seemed to want to concede that it was the festival itself that was to blame for their restlessness. The reason? It just didn't feel right.

Whether it was the timing, the rumour going round that claimed the *ricos* themselves had proposed the celebrations in their own honour, or the tension existing between the Jaeger-men and the two tall Arizonans — whom many folks now believed had come here hunting the dons' strong man and protector — nobody seemed sure. Some even claimed the tension was attributable to the strong rumour circulating that the maverick Espado planned a huge anti-dons demonstration during the festivities.

Just a few phlegmatic ones blamed it all on the heat.

Mostly Cobb himself could prove as unflappable as a Mayan stone statue. Not tonight. His instincts were clamouring; this wasn't the way he'd figured the manhunt would evolve. He knew he wouldn't close his eyes even if he downed a pint of snakehead whiskey.

So he did the only sensible thing a man could do. He went for a ride.

He was five miles out along the valley trail with a cool breeze blowing the cobwebs away when he heard the sound of someone following. Cutting off the trail into a clump of hackberries, he hauled his .45 and watched steely-eyed until the horseman hove into view. Then he swore, hammered down and kicked the sorrel back on to the trail.

'What the tarnation — ? he began, but Freeman held up a placating hand.

'Relax,' he grinned. 'I'm not playing nursemaid. I just got curious when you took off, is all.' He gestured. 'You heading anyplace in particular?'

'Nope.'

'Yet this is the trail to the valley.'

'So?'

'You weren't. Were you, Arizona?'

'Weren't what?'

'Fixing to try and threadneedle your way through the nighthawks up to Top Valley to find out if Jaeger was at home?' Freeman shook his head. 'No, not even old Pappy Cobb's mule-stubborn son would come up with a crazy notion like that.'

Their stares locked and held. Cobb realized, without even having framed the decision in his mind, that this *was* most likely what he'd intended. With days of tension in back of them, with their only tantalizing glimpses of the man they were hunting obtained from a distance, and with Jaeger under guard each time he appeared, he realized at last that he'd been building up to something and suddenly it had come to a head.

He was less eager to settle accounts with their killer now than just to get it all over and done with.

Or simply get himself killed? whispered a nagging inner voice.

Freeman interpreted his silence correctly. He understood, showed it by not commenting or losing his temper. For behind his unruffled façade the senior partner in this manhunting crew was every bit as suspicious, edgy and spoiling for action as Cobb.

Only thing, Luke Freeman knew he would toss in his grave for eternity if they went off half-cocked here and Jaeger took them down. He knew that, for all his impatience, Cobb would hate it even worse.

Understanding ran deep here despite events that had shattered a partnership. For in their day Freeman and Cobb had lived perilously close to the edge, had seen and survived greater perils than most men ever dreamed of, and there was a strength and understanding coming from that.

Together, in the early days, they'd fought Quahada Comanches during the last great breakouts, had buried ranchers who had been skinned and slowly roasted alive, whose screams could still be heard long, long after they had been laid in their graves.

Later, bossing their own big drives up from San Antone, the rivers had been flooded and Kiowas were on the rampage. They'd fought lightning, twister, stampede and heard the haunting Indian death-songs sung by the light of a Comanche moon, and had left the red man dead in his own whispering grass.

Experiences like that bonded people, and both seemed to be recalling such times in that long moment's silence before Freeman jerked a thumb northwest.

'They're all planning to be up all night at the sheep town. You know? Painting placards saying: 'Down with the Dons!' And Espado will be ranting up and down rehearsing his 'Free the Slaves!' speech.' He winked. 'And the girl . . . '

Cobb sat his saddle feeling his dangerous mood draining away. He almost managed a grin as he nodded in agreement and fell in behind Freeman, he clucked his horse into motion and pointed it back towards the high country and the sheep lands.

After about a mile, Cobb drew level.

'Much obliged,' he grunted.

'What are pards for?'

The big man thought that over as they climbed. Had the miles and the shared danger and frustration erased at last the scars that remained after Salvation Creek? Stranger things had happened, he supposed.

They rode through the moonlight until in the distance they heard a husky tequila voice bawling out passages from Lincoln's Gettysburg Address.

10

Dance of Death

The oom-pah-pah of trumpets erupting suddenly from in back of the tall-steepled church was the signal. Cheering erupted long before the crowd in the plaza could see anything of the parade, for there was plenty to be seen from right where they stood. The tradition of festivals and parades went far back into Ocotillo Province history, and if there were reservations about the reason for this occasion — or even the persistent rumour that Don Patricio himself had proposed the whole thing on a recommendation from Jaeger — this suddenly seemed of little or no importance. For life here, happy and simple once, had become a bitter and grinding thing to be endured in recent times. And if the poor Mexicans, the campesinos and the Indians who made up the work-force in the cruel valley could find in an occasion like this some little joy and forgetfulness, then what right had others to hold back? Let the excitement begin!

A skinny-legged child with skirts flying rushed in from Carrizo Avenue screaming: 'They come! They come!' and everybody cheered, even though nobody appeared for what seemed several long minutes.

There had been a hitch.

The Women of the Fallen Heroes had turned up in their numbers in white dresses and the red sashes which commemorated their men who'd perished in the last great battle with Cochise, insisting they should lead because the festival day fell close to the battle anniversary.

This honour was contested by the members of the Royal Spanish Marching Brigade of Ocotillo Province who felt their signal success in last January's parade in honour of the Pope entitled them to the distinction.

The noisy rag-tag squad towards the rear toting crudely painted banners demanding 'Equality for All!' and 'Suspend *Nuevos Rurales*!' set up an impatient, jeering howling and the situation appeared in danger of erupting before it had properly begun, when a tall figure rose majestically from the leading flower-bedecked coach and silenced the racket with a commanding gesture.

'Continue in the order we are in now!' decreed Don Patricio. Then turning his silver head, he added: 'Do you not agree, *muchachas*?'

Up until that point, such was the explosive atmosphere of excitement and antagonism that marchers and protesters hadn't seemed to notice the silent unobtrusive line of horsemen drawing up before the livery stables.

They noticed now.

The fading sunset glow glinted from the hard faces of the gringo gunmen from their weapons and harness. Most times the Jaegermen went about Grande Ronde in threes or fours. It was a long time since anybody had seen ten of them together. Now they looked anything but festive.

An uneasy silence fell and yet again the Great Festival of the Dons seemed at risk of dying stillborn. Then to the astonishment of all who knew him only as a chilling and remote figure, Kyle Jaeger heeled into sight from behind the line-up and waved his big hat — with a grin!

'Come on, *amigos*!' His booming voice carried easily over the crowded walks and rapidly filling plaza. 'We're here to march and play and get rolling damn drunk if we want. Why do you reckon we called for this celebration? We want folks to get along better, and you can start by marching and singing just like you've been rehearsing. Yessir, that's the programme, so what say we start right now!'

Was that a threat, or a plea?

Suddenly it didn't seem to matter

one way or the other. The blood-stirring combined voices of the trumpets filled the darkening sky to be supported immediately by fiddles and guitars chiming in lustily, and suddenly all were rolling exuberantly forward in a surging flood of colour, noise and good-natured energy.

The uncertain moment was over and the excitement seemed all the greater for that small hitch as the parade swung into the square. Immediately the first fireworks took to the sky, seemingly boosted all the higher by the sheer volume of the applause that greeted the spectacle.

Hail to the padre, marching at the vanguard, so impressive in his flowing robes! Hail to the musicians, the marchers who'd taken such pains with their costumes! And even the ragged, wild-eyed discredited phalanx of banner-waving objectors and protesters, who, even if certain to cause trouble as usual before the day was out, were still heroes to many. And — what the hell — this was fiesta day — so hail to the dons themselves, even if they were just a pack of blood-sucking vampires feeding upon the pure and holy blood of the poor!

All hail!

Off to such a zestful start the evening quickly gathered momentum with performing entertainers, exhibitions of startling horsemanship, food and drink of every variety available in seemingly unending quantities, and with only the occasional brawl or flash of a knife to keep the *Rurales* busy.

Two men watched the excited ebb and flow below their lofty position in the flag room of the Placita Hotel, unsmiling, not celebrating, never taking their eyes from the preening dons or the swaggering Jaegermen who seemed as removed from the spirit of the event as themselves; the occasional glimpse of the man they were committed to confront before the last trumpet sounded.

The day the festival had been

announced the partners had made the vow that if they hadn't avenged the boys of the Strolling B beforehand, they must accomplish the deed on this day or admit defeat.

The waiting time had been brutally testing.

There had been occasions here in town when Jaeger had ridden by within easy sixgun range. Yet not once had they been tempted. For every single time they'd glimpsed their quarry at either close or far range, he was accompanied by anything between seven and ten *pistoleros*. Sure, they could make a try — and end up dead. They wanted him but not that bad.

But time now was running out fast.

It would be tonight, they agreed as shadows began to lengthen, flares were lighted and the square below swarmed with dancers, jugglers, drinkers, musicians, protesters, pretty girls and scores of the sad-happy poor in their Sunday best, all now determined to have a fine time before tomorrow's dawn found them again bending their backs under the farmlanders' whips.

'He's gotta figure we're waiting our chance,' Cobb growled as they watched Jaeger quietly steering his appaloosa through the boisterous crowds to make his unhurried way towards the flower-bedecked dais in the north-west corner.

Freeman nodded soberly. He interpreted the fact that Jaeger had not come after them personally before this as evidence that the killer had a bigger game to play, although what that might be they couldn't begin to guess. Nothing else made sense. He'd risked his hide trying to kill them at Pierro Pass, yet apart from a couple of skirmishes with his hellions here, had since let them be.

He knew one thing. He wouldn't be taking his eyes off the man until he actually had him in his gunsights. And, rubbing the back of his neck, he wondered why, with everything appearing so normal and even buoyant below them — even to the occasional boisterous brawls breaking out between Espado's people and the *Nuevos* — why this constant nagging sensation that he was missing something vital and dangerous that he really should be able to see?

★   ★   ★

The stage was set for terror.

Jaeger's heavy-lidded eyes blinked slowly in the gathering shadows, and his dark heart kicked with anticipation.

Directly before him the *Nuevos* and his men were casually taking up their appointed positions around and upon the dais, the dons beaming and making small talk as they also prepared to mount the sturdy plank steps up to their high places and their doom.

From the day he'd returned from California to take up where he'd left off with Patricio, the scene had existed vividly in his mind; now it had become reality.

It had had to be this way.

To achieve his goals the dons must die, but not in such a way that blame could ever be directed at him. He'd structured events so that the don-hating Espado — already raising hell and spouting anti-don slogans — would be the natural suspect for the atrocity. Jaeger's *Nuevos* were programmed to ensure that the old rebel would be accused, convicted and either gunned down or executed in quick time — leaving Kyle Jaeger unscathed, unsuspected and ready to fill the power vacuum the dead would leave in the valley.

It would be brutal and bloody with a degree of risk of things going wrong, but he could already taste his triumph.

He glanced around sharply as though suddenly feeling eyes boring into him. He shrugged. He saw only a sea of happy faces, along with faces filled with hate, the faces of the haves and have-nots. But no lethal faces. But his men and the *Nuevos* all had their orders once the don-deed was done.

The dons first, then Freeman and Cobb. He glanced up to the first stars dusting the night sky behind the darkened hotel tower room.

★   ★   ★

Torches and streetlamps were being lit and a murmur of expectancy swept the *placita*. Drunks began to sing, a pretty girl danced and swayed spontaneously before the dais where important men were gathering. Then yet another mêlée involving Espado, Gallardo and a bunch of overseers from the valley erupted directly in front of the cantina, but it quickly petered out.

Now the crowds began converging around the dais and *Rurales* and gunmen moved smartly into position the moment a lavishly ornamented carriage bearing the three dons showed again. The great men had been taken off to the club following their initial appearance, to feast and wine in style before exposing themselves to the rabble again. Seated together and waving from the high seat, they appeared to be in genuinely high spirits as they made their regal way through the throng.

With a bitter taste in his mouth from too many cigarettes, Cobb growled:

'How'll we do it after this circus shuts down? We go after him or wait for him to come after us? He's here, he's got more gunnies with him than you can poke a stick at, he knows we're about — just as he's gotta know that the longer he takes the higher the risk we'll get to him first. He'll come after us, which will give us the advantage, don't you figure?'

But Freeman's expression was distant now, thoughtful. He leaned on the railing and glanced up at Cobb speculatively.

'What do you plan doing after we get back?'

'Same as before. I've got a drive lined up.'

'You recall me talking to that rancher

outside Nogales on our way down?'

Cobb nodded absently. He was watching the scene below. The dons were mounting the dais for the speeches, flanked by *vaqueros*, not Jaegermen. Freeman went on: 'He wanted to sell two hundred head — '

'They were in poor condition.'

'Sure. But do you recollect what the country was like between Nogales and Durant?'

'Sure. Green from the unseasonal rains. Why?'

'That shirt-tail rancher doesn't know that. We could get the cows for a song, graze them on the new grass all the way north, put about two hundred pounds on every head then sell them as prime in Albuquerque.'

Now Cobb was concentrating. He realized that Freeman's proposal made sense. But what impressed far more was that the man who'd once been his partner was suggesting they pard up again. That made him feel good for the first time in a long and testing day. But it was a good feeling that was not destined to last.

They returned to the scene below where the dons now preened from their flower-bedecked chairs upon the high dais and waved and smiled at the people they oppressed.

Hatred came back at them in waves but the *ricos* were accustomed to that. This event was calculated to remind the have-nots of their power, and that power was represented in part by the hated *Nuevos Rurales* now standing at ground level with backs to the dais, forming a living protective barricade.

In addition, the dons' rear was protected by a number of hand-picked *vaqueros* wearing flat-brimmed black hats, and guns. On the ground behind the dais in the space between the structure and the supplies store stood one more row of hard faces and double gunrigs.

The Jaegermen were there in force and their leader was with them.

The speeches had just begun when a

big man high above noticed something.

'Look,' he growled. 'Jaeger's gone.'

Staring intently, Freeman realized it was so. And even as they watched the Jaegermen were silently and smoothly easing back away from their position at the rear of the dais, filing to vanish through the doorway of the utility store some thirty feet distant.

'What . . . ?' a puzzled Freeman began. He broke off as a crouching figure emerged from beneath the dais, a figure with broad shoulders and fiery red hair who also moved swiftly to make for the storeroom.

From the darkness below the dais, a flickering light and a sinister tendril of blue smoke.

'Tierney . . . ' Cobb began, then broke off abruptly as they found themselves staring down at something they couldn't comprehend, at first. They saw the dais and the figures crowded upon it appear to rise slowly at first, then surge faster and higher until they realized that the great weight of people and the platform were riding upon a swelling ball of livid fire that preceded the insane thunderclap of the explosion which momentarily sent a thousand people deaf.

Then the screaming began.

★   ★   ★

The hotel's outside steps delivered them to ground level at the fringe of the chaotic crowd. The scene was total madness, the noise overwhelming. But Cobb's stentorian roar was louder and angrier.

'It was Jaeger!' he thundered, punching a shot into the sky.

'We saw Tierney light the dynamite and — hey! There they are now! There's the bombers. Look!'

For an instant, dimly recognizable through the smoke and flames of the dais, Wolf Tierney and Jaeger, ranged up against the storeroom wall in back of the conflagration, seemed to freeze like wild animals caught in a spotlight as the mass of faces seemed to turn into a sea of accusing eyes. The plan had been for them to hide from the explosion in the utility room then emerge to 'help'.

In that hanging moment, Espado leapt atop a display stand.

'I also see the Tierney, *amigos*,' he hollered. 'He does this godless thing. Jaeger does it. Seize them!

Freeman and Cobb took up the chant as they went ploughing through the mob with guns held high, the white rage masking their faces impossible to deny. The mob wanted something to vent their hysteria upon, and suddenly they had it. There was a surging rumbling roar of voices and there were angry surging figures ahead of the Arizonans when the sixguns opened up.

Panicked by the mob and unable to be checked by Jaeger, the gunfighters were lashing back.

Freeman leapt over a smouldering log on the bloodstained cobblestones which was actually the bomb-blasted body of Don D'Palma. His .45 was in his hand and he lurched through the smoke haze. In close to the dais it was a scene straight out of Hades with dead and dying strewn across the corner of the plaza over twenty yards and more. Invisible mouths were screaming or cursing, the cobblestones glistening with blood, madness ran amok.

He was almost knocked off his feet by a staggering figure blinded by the blast. Then he heard someone shout:

'It was them stinking sheepers! Espado! We knew he was planning something. Get Espado! Get them dirty rebels!'

Freeman turned his head. Cobb was tagging him through the nightmare. He moved towards the sound of shouting and suddenly through the haze came face to face with the desperate shouting Jaegerman who was attempting to stem the tide and shift the blame.

A gun roared behind him and the Jaegerman was flung backward into burning débris with a sudden third eye in his forehead.

Cobb was at his side with a smoking gun.

'What . . . ?'

It was all the big man was able to get out before the dim figure of Jaeger appeared in a window of the storeroom brandishing a smoking gun and howling in a voice that dominated even the madness.

'There they are, boys! The bastards that tried to murder me in Pierro — pards of Espado! Freeman and Cobb! They tried to kill me and now they've killed half the town. Take 'em down, *amigos*!'

It was another desperate ploy that didn't take. As shock receded the mob was focusing single-mindedly upon the hated Jaegermen, and at that vital moment Espado and Gallardo came surging round the flank of the dais with a dozen smoke-grimed 'rebels' behind them.

'Charge, *compañeros*!' Espado screamed excitedly. 'For freedom and justice and — ' A bullet knocked him down.

But three men took his place. Two of them fell. The deadly enemy was forting up in the storeroom. Freeman and Cobb cut loose at shadowy figures running for the storeroom, then dived to ground as murderous fire came lashing back. Through the crash of gunfire could be heard Jaeger's bull voice bawling orders and his henchmen were responding as they always had done.

There was no telling how many hellions survived to make it into the stout-walled storeroom whose windows were immediately illuminated by the scorching flare of their defensive fire.

The first volley was vicious and the frenzied mob was being carved up from cover. The Arizonans managed to get shoulder to shoulder as a rifle stormed and a bullet whipped over their heads. Cobb shot a Jaegerman down, then ducked low as a flung missile whipped close overhead. They were trapped in a vortex of human hysteria — and lethal fire continued to pour from the besieged storeroom.

Was Jaeger's firepower going to carry the day after all?

Freeman jolted Cobb with his elbow and jerked his head at the cantina which faced the storeroom across some sixty feet of lethal open space. They leapt up and ran with whining messengers of death threatening their every step. The ugly sound of bullets thudding into living flesh and bone all about them lent wings to their feet.

The cantina loomed abruptly out of the smoke. They charged directly through the swinging doors of the Spanish Rose, a bullet following them smashing bar mirrors as a half-dozen white-faced citizens vanished through the rear doors at sight of them. They made a fearsome sight, smoke-darkened, snarling, bristling with guns.

Freeman triggered out the lights and Cobb shot dead a broad-shouldered Jaegerman with a bloodied shoulder when he appeared in a high window next to the door behind a cocked revolver.

The corpse hung over the sill. Cries of rage and hysteria rose from the *placita* outside.

Crouched in the semi-darkness the two reloaded in record time and traded glances. No words. None was needed. It was the cattle-drovers versus the Kiowas all over again. You didn't talk. You saved everything you had and you aimed to kill with every bullet.

The Jaegermen were getting their range.

A window exploded and shards of glass shot across the room like daggers. One sank into Cobb's shoulder. He plucked it out and blood spurted. Freeman's sixers bellowed twice and a silhouette in a window howled in agony and brought up his guts on the way to the floor. One less Jaegerman. But another filled his place. The enemy was cool and now had the angry mob receding and ducking for cover from their accurate fire. Just as they'd been trained.

A lone voice urged his fellow citizens on.

'Fight on, *amigos*! Our *compañeros* from Arizona need us to help — ' The crash of a revolver drowned out Espado's cry.

There was no counting time. The vicious gun duel flaring across the deadly space separating cantina and storeroom might have raged for five minutes or fifty before a sudden hush fell on the plaza. A single rifle shot sounded, followed by an authoritative voice which sounded vaguely familiar:

'Cease in the name of the *Federales*! You are all in contempt of the law. The next man to offend will hang, I promise you!'

Freeman and Cobb lowered their guns and picked their way across the littered cantina floor to reach the window where the dead man hung. The scene before them was a war zone. The smoke had almost cleared and the remnants of the mob who had stayed to fight on now swung about, gaping at something beyond. Squinting through the haze the Arizonans suddenly sighted the squad of mounted horsemen with rifles in their hands sporting grey uniforms and black billed caps.

Federalistas!

They knuckled their eyes, then glimpsed the small erect figure astride a high-shouldered dun — and it was like history repeating itself for the two slack-jawed Arizonans.

Captain Melgosa looked every inch in total command of the situation as he lifted his sabre high.

'I returned because I smelt trouble, and how terribly right I was. Throw down your weapons and disperse instantly or I assure you the full weight of the law will fall upon each and everyone of you. I speak for the *Federales*! I am the *Federales*, and the *Federales* are Mexico!'

They believed him. And the authority of the *Federales*, rarely seen this far north, was still unchallengeable. Already weapons were being lowered and Freeman and Cobb were slack-jawed as they realized just how many had been slain or wounded in the murderous affray. But there was still an angry mob in the background, and suddenly they were shouting — bawling a welcome to the *Federales* and howling denunciations that weren't clear at first until the runty bloodied figure of Espado appeared, draped in a 'No Slavery!' banner.

'Great *Capitán*!' he called hoarsely. 'They murdered the dons!' He twisted and jabbed an accusing finger towards the ruined dais and the bullet-pocked storeroom beyond. 'Jaeger and his butchers! They stand accused. They were seen lighting the dynamite. They slew one of those who saw, but there are two more who — '

A .45 roared from the storeroom and the runty figure tumbled. Instantly the crowd responded, chanting hysterically and brandishing stakes and weapons as they charged blindly.

At first a disbelieving Jaeger began triggering into the sky to try and stem the tide. It was impossible. The mob had scented the true beast and not even the *Federales* could hold them back as Gallardo and Juanita led the rebels into the attack.

Such was the force of the human tide that Freeman and Cobb knew they would be swept aside if they tried to stop it. That didn't prevent them from trying, and, as expected, they proved ineffectual. An apparently immortal Espado was back on his feet, urging them on — the passion of his years of oppression and frustration transferring to his people.

Jaeger couldn't believe any of it — how it had all gone so wrong — the sixgun ferocity of Freeman and Cobb — the lion courage of grubby little Espado and his sub-humans — the captain. None of it. From the back of the smoke-filled room he kept shooting and shouting, calling on Melgosa to take action against the hysterical men and women now crashing repeatedly against the storeroom walls. But the numbers were too great and an ashen-faced Melgosa could not bring himself to order gunfire against 'the shirtless ones'.

Grim and relentless now, Cobb and Freeman quit the cantina and ran to the storeroom wall, were trying to fight their way along to the door when a peasant ahead of them bobbed up and blasted a shot through a window.

The single bullet ricocheted off a keg and whined across the storeroom to shatter a heavy glass container upon a high shelf. The four-gallon container was filled with coal-oil used by the lamp-lighter. The flare of the shot touched off by the towering figure crouched directly below caused the downpour to ignite as it engulfed the man instantly from head to toe.

In one incandescent moment Jaeger was transformed from a man into a staggering, arms-akimbo figure from out of a nightmare with flames leaping upwards from every inch of him, only his eyes — twin orbs of horror — identifiable in his melting face as he crashed blindly into the double doors which burst open before his weight.

Half the mob shrieked in horror, half was struck dumb as the monstrous apparition blazed its blind way along the plankwalk which was illuminated bright as day for an interminable slice of time before the figure came crashing down full length upon the boards. One arm lifted as though beckoning for help, then froze in that position as the now motionless figure blackened and appeared to shrink within its own fluttering cocoon of fire.

The plaza was now still.

★   ★   ★

They were eager to ride but it seemed that might not be possible. At first. The captain was standing his ground. Having already questioned the Arizonans, the surviving Jaegermen, Espado and his people along with the *Nuevos Rurales*, who would very shortly become ex-*Nuevos* under a new administration planned for Grande Ronde, Melgosa now believed he had at least a broad picture of what had happened here.

But thorough to a meticulous degree, he insisted there was much he still did not understand, and therefore must satisfy himself before anybody quit.

Everybody turned to stare at Tierney. Shot in the shoulder and leg during the gun battle, Tierney had been Jaeger's *segundo* as everyone knew, including the captain. If anyone could fill in the details of the why and how the dons had been murdered, it had to be the redheaded *pistolero*.

But an ashen and agonized Tierney could already feel the bite of the hangrope, and continued to stall until a practical captain assured him of 'merely' a life sentence if he co-operated.

Then he sang like a bird.

All but two listeners were absorbed by the story of how Jaeger had deliberately set out to win over the dons, unite them to make them an easier target, and helped them enslave the peons — with his own future status of lord of the valley in mind. He'd then set about to destroy them in one fell swoop and lay the blame upon the rebels after which he would have seized control over Saragoza Valley as he'd seen others do in the goldfields of California.

Every listener knew he was hearing the truth at last.

Cobb and Freeman were mounting up as the captain and the sheepfarmers gathered to make their goodbyes. The two seemed distant and preoccupied as they started off a short time later. Their thoughts and emotions were no longer centered here, but back in New Mexico.

'You reckon the boys would be resting easy at last now?' Cobb asked as their horses carried them towards the place along the flame-scorched walk where the stiff and blackened corpse still lay upon the seared porchboards exactly as it had fallen.

Freeman did not answer immediately. They reined in to study the motionless

figure. Then he glanced across at Cobb.
Both nodded. There was an ending
here.

They rode from the town.

THE END

We do hope that you have enjoyed reading this large print book.

Did you know that all of our titles are available for purchase?

We publish a wide range of high quality large print books including:
Romances, Mysteries, Classics
General Fiction
Non Fiction and Westerns

Special interest titles available in large print are:
The Little Oxford Dictionary
Music Book, Song Book
Hymn Book, Service Book

Also available from us courtesy of Oxford University Press:
Young Readers' Dictionary
(large print edition)
Young Readers' Thesaurus
(large print edition)

For further information or a free brochure, please contact us at:
Ulverscroft Large Print Books Ltd.,
The Green, Bradgate Road, Anstey,
Leicester, LE7 7FU, England.
Tel: (00 44) **0116 236 4325**
Fax: (00 44) **0116 234 0205**

BLADE LAW

Jack Reason

A silver necklet was all that was left to identify the body of the man McKee found dead in the mountains. The brutal murder was the work of Juan Darringo and his bandits who had made the mountain ranges their lair of robbery and death . . . However, identification of the dead man was to lead McKee back to the mountains accompanied by a man intent on retribution. Now, forced to pit their wits against the cruel terrain, they also find themselves the prey in a hunt that will have only one outcome.